BUDDY MAKES A DECISION.

"I've decided I need a son. I'm going to hire a surrogate mother and raise the kid myself. And I don't want just anybody for the mother. She's got to be the right size, the right temperature."

BUDDY ASKS A GIRLFRIEND.

They had a lovely evening together. Buddy remembered the part about the rain the best because it reminded him of the umbrella. The umbrella that Emily kept hitting him with . . .

BUDDY INTERVIEWS A PROFESSIONAL.

"While we're on the subject of hair, Miss Werner, we might discuss the mat on the top of your head. Do you shampoo or do you crop dust?"

BUDDY MEETS THE PERFECT MOTHER.

"What's your name?" There was a quiver in his voice.
"Maggie."
Buddy swallowed. "Maggie, I'd like to ask you to have my child. Well? What do you say?"
"All right," she agreed. "Fifty thousand dollars."

PATERNITY

CHARLIE PETERS

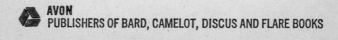
AVON
PUBLISHERS OF BARD, CAMELOT, DISCUS AND FLARE BOOKS

PATERNITY is an original publication of Avon Books. This work has never before appeared in book form.

AVON BOOKS
A division of
The Hearst Corporation
959 Eighth Avenue
New York, New York 10019

Published by arrangement with Charlie Peters Films, Inc. and Paramount Pictures Corporation
Library of Congress Catalog Card Number: 81-66462
ISBN: 0-380-78527-7

First Avon Printing, October, 1981

PATERNITY

ONE

BUDDY EVANS HAD IT ALL. LOOKS. CHARM. PERSONALITY.
A high paying job. An apartment on the Upper East
Side. A good tailor. No alimony. Men liked him. Women
adored him.

You'd never guess there was something missing in his
life. But something was. Something that even Buddy
himself couldn't put his finger on.

Like many other people, Buddy Evans was a creature
of habit. Every weekday morning, he awoke at seven
sharp. Two-mile jog around the park. Shower, shave,
dress. Then a long, brisk walk to Woodson's Coffee
Shop on East Thirty-fourth Street, picking up the morning *Times* along the way from Sid the vendor.

Once inside Woodson's, he went directly to his own
personal booth where he was joined every morning by
his friend and colleague Kurt Stearns.

Every morning but *this* morning.

Buddy glanced at his watch. Eight-thirty. Kurt was
half an hour late. Buddy's stomach growled at him. He
turned to the sports page and decided to give the bastard
another five minutes.

"Happy birthday to you . . ."

Buddy chuckled but did not look up. Somebody was
singing "Happy Birthday" to some poor slob in the

7

restaurant. How embarrassing. He scanned Red Smith's column.

"Happy birthday to you . . ."

The voice was coming closer. Buddy sneaked a look over the top of his paper and caught a glimpse of someone in bright yellow coming his way. He went back to Red Smith.

"Happy birthday, Buddy Evans . . ."

Buddy Evans?! Buddy pulled the paper away and was confronted by a mass of moving yellow feathers. The feathers were attached to a costume, and the costume was being worn by a small man with an idiotic expression on his face, peering out from beneath a cap with a brim designed to look like the bill of a bird.

"Mr. Evans?"

The guy was dressed as a chicken! Buddy grimaced.

"Mr. *Buddy* Evans?"

"Uh . . . yes," Buddy replied, suddenly aware that everyone in the restaurant was looking in his direction. He realized that *he* was the poor slob.

"Just wanted to make sure," the chicken man said with a silly smile. And with that, he cleared his throat and started "Happy Birthday" all over again.

The realization hit Buddy Evans like a slap in the face. He was forty-four years old today. He knew this because a chicken was singing "Happy Birthday" to him in a restaurant in midtown Manhattan.

The chicken man hopped up on a chair and began to flap his wings up and down as he continued to sing. Buddy felt trapped. He sank into the booth as low as was humanly possible. His handsome face lost no time in turning crimson with embarrassment.

After the chicken man had reprised the number three times, the people in the surrounding booths good-naturedly joined in for the finale.

"Happy birthday, dear Budd-eeeeee"—everybody in the place knew his name by now thanks to the idiot in the chicken suit—"Happy birthday to youuuuuuuu . . ."

A hearty round of applause followed.

Buddy stood up and smiled politely. He tipped the chicken man five dollars, graciously accepted congratulations from the strangers around him, thrust some money in the direction of the cashier, and got the hell out.

He found Kurt outside on the sidewalk, convulsed with laughter.

"You shoulda seen your face," Kurt howled, leaning against a mailbox for support. "I watched through the window!"

Buddy's first impulse was to strangle him, but he quickly remembered that he'd pulled worse stunts himself. Buddy shook his head and grinned.

"Okay," Buddy said, "you've had your little fun."

Kurt wiped a tear from his eye. "I should've hired somebody with a movie camera," he said.

Kurt caught his breath and regarded Buddy soberly. Then he burst out laughing again.

"Come on, laughing boy." Buddy took him by the arm. "We're gonna be late for work."

He steered his friend toward Eighth Avenue.

"Thanks for remembering my birthday," Buddy said with an evil glint in his eye. "Next year, I'm gonna be sure to remember *yours*."

Buddy Evans and Kurt Stearns were a genuine odd couple. Though only a few years older than Buddy, Kurt looked at least ten years older. He'd given up trying to retain the look and shape of his youth long ago, although his wife Evelyn was constantly coercing him into diet and exercise regimens—none of which had the slightest effect on him. Whereas Buddy was tall and trim, Kurt was short and stocky. Whereas Buddy was always the first person people noticed in a crowd, Kurt was generally the last. Whereas Buddy was always immaculately dressed and groomed, Kurt always looked as if he'd spent the night in his clothes. "Rumpled" described him best. But whereas Buddy's gaze tended to be misinterpreted as regal and aloof, Kurt's was unmistakably open and friendly. People had a tendency to underestimate Kurt, and Kurt counted on that. As a lawyer, he'd always been able to turn that fact to his advantage. Kurt was a damned good lawyer and highly respected in his field.

They say that opposites attract. Buddy and Kurt were living proof of that. As undergraduates at Fordham over twenty years ago, they'd hit it off immediately. Though different in countless ways—Kurt the family man, Buddy the irresponsible playboy—what they did share, outside of a genuine affection for one another, was the same sense of humor. They were constantly playing elaborate practical jokes on each other, as evidenced by Buddy's recent encounter with the singing chicken.

As they turned the next corner, Buddy caught sight of something that stopped him in his tracks. First the chicken man. Now this.

Kurt started chuckling. Madison Square Garden's electronic marquee was spelling out "Happy Birthday, Buddy Evans" in bright red letters. You could see it for blocks.

Kurt nudged his friend. "I almost told Rudy to put up 'Happy Forty-fourth,' but I figured you wouldn't want all your girlfriends to know how old you really are."

Buddy shook his head and began to laugh. He turned to Kurt and put an arm around his shoulder. "I'll get you for this," he promised.

"I knew you'd like it."

"But please tell Rudy to take it off," Buddy instructed. "It's embarrassing." He looked around at the mystified pedestrians who were staring up at the marquee.

"Forty-four." Kurt shook his head and let out a low whistle. "Living on borrowed time, Buddy."

Buddy frowned at him. "We're late," he said.

As they passed through the main doors of Madison Square Garden, Buddy felt suddenly invigorated. Forty-four? Hell, he felt *twenty*-four. The Garden had this effect on him practically every morning. Running this place was like having the Fountain of Youth at your disposal. Over the hill? Not Buddy Evans. Not the playboy of the Western Hemisphere.

"You know," Kurt said in somber tones as they approached the main floor, "forty-four is when it hit *me*."

"When *what* hit you?"

"My morality."

"You mean your mor*tality*."

"Uh-uh. My morality. Hit me like a brick."

"If you've got any more birthday surprises lined up, *I'm* gonna hit you like a brick," Buddy promised. He waved to the ticketman as they passed his booth.

"No more surprises," Kurt assured him. "But listen, let me tell you what happened to me when I turned forty-four."

Buddy groaned. "Have I got a choice?"

"I woke up one morning," Kurt began, "and suddenly realized that I had nothing to leave behind. I said to myself, 'Kurt Stearns, you are an incomplete man.' That's what I said."

"Why are you trying to depress me?" Buddy asked.

"Because you're forty-four years old. You can't be happy *all* your life."

"Who says I'm happy?"

"You're the most eligible bachelor in Manhattan. A different girl every night. How could you *not* be happy?"

Buddy ignored him. They entered the arena where a boxing ring was under construction. Buddy stopped and shouted to the workmen, "Make sure you leave enough space under the ropes for Forry to crawl out through!"

The workmen laughed. One of them, the foreman, shouted back, "Forry's gonna whip that Cuban's ass!"

Buddy dug into his pocket and pulled out a twenty-dollar bill. He waved it at the foreman. The foreman pulled a twenty out of his own pocket and waved it back. "You're on, Mr. Evans," he called. "Even if it *is* my whole week's salary!"

Buddy laughed and hurried to catch up with Kurt who was holding one of the elevators. As Buddy hopped in and the doors swished shut, Kurt appraised him mournfully.

"Some day," Kurt remarked in prophetic tones, "you're gonna be old and unhappy. And you won't even know it."

"Yes, I will," Buddy replied. "You'll be around to remind me."

Buddy's outer office was a beehive of activity and confusion. Iris, Buddy's middle-aged secretary, shoved her Harlequin Romance under the desk blotter as he approached.

"Happy birthday, Mr. Evans," she said, not mustering much enthusiasm. "The Human Vise is in your office."

Buddy gave her a quizzical look.

"The wrestler," she explained.

"Oh. *That* Human Vise."

Out of the corner of his eye, Buddy saw a small gray blur streaking across the carpet, headed straight for him. He knew immediately who it was and broke into a wide grin.

"Oh, my god!" Buddy pretended to look around for an avenue of escape. "It's Whiplash Wilson!"

His path was instantly blocked by a tiny middle-aged man in a shabby, salt-and-pepper suit and an equally unattractive porkpie hat, clutching a tattered briefcase under one arm. He was already going into his rehearsed spiel. "Mr. Evans, I am here representing Mrs. Herman Kupferberg who is seeking financial remuneration for injuries sustained—"

"Hey, Whiplash," Kurt interrupted from the doorway to his office. "How come *you* never get injured?"

Whiplash was nearly impossible to derail once he got started. "—sustained on these grounds during a New York Knickerbockers basketball game—"

Buddy just stood there and pretended to listen attentively to the high-pitched drone. Whiplash had been a Garden fixture for years, even before Buddy had come to work there. In all that time, he had never once succeeded in getting a settlement for any of his cockeyed cases. Buddy sometimes wondered how the little shyster managed to support himself. Whiplash was always underfoot, hanging around the offices, haunting the hallways with his beady eyes peeled for any calamity that might be twisted into a lawsuit. Although it would have been easy enough for Buddy to have him barred from the premises, he had actually developed a soft spot for the little character. Some days he actually looked forward to the crazed yammering. He even missed Whiplash on days he didn't show up.

"Mr. Evans," Iris called from her desk. "The Human Vise? He's waiting."

"Right, right, the Human Vise," Buddy said and laid a hand on Whiplash's shoulder. "Why don't we discuss this a little later, Whiplash? I've got a real busy schedule today."

Whiplash was still going strong. "—these injuries sustained to Mrs. Kupferberg's body include—"

Buddy deftly moved around the jabbering little man and entered his office, shutting the door behind him. He leaned back against the closed door and smiled. Whiplash Wilson, he thought to himself. What would the day be like without him?

Buddy loved his office. He loved the deep-pile carpeting and the warm, low lighting. He loved the framed pictures of sports figures past and present on the wall. He loved his video wall. But most of all he loved the huge one-way window behind his desk that looked down on the main floor of the Garden—his kingdom.

"Mr. Evans?"

Across the room, a huge hulking figure detached itself from the couch and approached.

It was a man. Maybe. It looked more like a gorilla somebody had forced into a three-piece suit.

"Mr. Evans." The voice was barely Homo sapiens. "I'm the Human Vise."

The Human Vise extended something vaguely resembling a hand. Buddy shook it—carefully.

"I have a scheduling problem," the wrestler explained. "You see, I have a tag-team match with the Toro Brothers on April 16, but unfortunately, I also have a philosophy exam at the New School on that same day."

Buddy stepped away from the door and regarded him with disbelief. "Philosophy exam?"

Whiplash suddenly burst into the office. "—spasms of the lower back resulting in fluctuations of the calf—"

"Uh, Whiplash," Buddy interjected. He could feel a headache brewing. "We're trying to have a meeting here . . ."

Whiplash kept jabbering away.

"Mr. Vise," Buddy called out to the wrestler over Whiplash. "Would you do me a big favor and escort Mr. Wilson here out? I promise to take care of the scheduling problem."

"Sure thing, Mr. Evans."

The Human Vise walked over to Whiplash, picked him up, tucked him under one arm, and walked out of the office.

Whiplash didn't miss a beat. "—as well as major and minor contusions in various other areas of the body—"

Buddy shut and locked the door. He could feel his forehead tightening. It was all Kurt's doing. All that business about turning forty-four. He crossed the room to his desk and pushed a button on the intercom. "Iris," he said. "Come in, Iris. Over."

A deep voice replied. "What is it, your highness?"

"Iris, what's wrong with your voice?" Buddy asked in surprise.

"It's not Iris, it's Kurt. Iris had to step out."

"Well, when she gets back, would you tell her I don't want any interruptions or calls, please?"

"What's the matter?"

"You. You're the matter. You've given me a headache with all that over-the-hill jazz."

"What did I say?" Kurt asked innocently. "It's your birthday, Buddy. You should be happy."

"Then why'd you tell me I was incomplete?" Buddy wanted to know. "Look, just tell Iris I don't want to be disturbed for about an hour, okay?"

"But there's somebody here who wants to see you."

"I'm not seeing *any*body."

"Not even Tad?"

"Tad?" Buddy's face lit up. Kurt's ten-year-old son. Just the tonic he needed. "I'll be right out," Buddy said excitedly. "Tell him we're gonna shoot some baskets."

And not three minutes later, Buddy and Tad were down on the main floor, tossing basketballs at one of the hoops Buddy had instructed the workmen to bring out. Tad was only ten, but already he was a terror with the ball. The kid could really hit.

"How come you're not in school today?" Buddy asked him.

"It's Elias Howe Day," Tad replied, executing a successful hook shot.

"I'm forty-four today," Buddy stated matter-of-factly. "It's my birthday."

He waited for the boy's response. Tad tucked the basketball under one arm and stared at Buddy in an uncomprehending manner. "Forty-four years *old*?" he asked.

Buddy nodded. Tad raised an eyebrow in surprise.

"How old did you think I was?"

"Not *that* old."

"Tell me something, Tad. Do I look like an incomplete man to you? Your dad says I'm incomplete."

Tad's mind was still lagging a few steps behind. "I had a teacher once," the boy remarked. "I think he was forty-*three*. His name was Mr. Collins."

Tad walked over to the foul line and prepared to shoot.

Buddy hustled over beneath the backboard to await Tad's shot. "Tell me something," he said. "This Mr. Collins. Is *he* incomplete?"

"No. He's dead."

Tad shot. Swish. Perfect.

"He died of a heart attack."

Buddy didn't even feel it when the basketball bounced off his head. "Forty-*three*?" He couldn't believe it. "A heart attack at forty-*three*?"

"He was my gym teacher." Tad retrieved the ball and dribbled back to the foul line. "One day in class he got into the sit-up position and that was it. We thought he was kidding at first."

Shoulders sagging, Buddy left the court and walked over to the bleachers. He sat down and watched Tad take a few more shots, but his mind was no longer on basketball. It was on his own mortality. Sensing Buddy's worry, Tad came over and sat down beside him.

"Uncle Buddy," the boy said sympathetically, "I'm no expert on this stuff, but maybe you ought to get married."

Buddy looked at Tad, surprised by his statement. "I *was* married," Buddy told him. "Once. A long time ago. But it didn't work out. Totally my fault. I had this one bad habit."

"What was that?"

"I kept finding her in bed with other guys."

Tad giggled and Buddy laughed. He put his arm around the boy. "I'm just kidding," he admitted. "It was a lot more complicated than that. Anyway, the last thing that good old Uncle Buddy needs is to get married. I need . . . something . . . something else."

"Like what?" Tad waggled his eyebrows Groucho-style. "Sex?"

"No. Not sex." He smiled at Tad. "I'll tell you one thing, though. I wish I had a son like you."

"That's why I think you ought to get married," Tad explained. "You'd make a *great* dad."

Buddy nodded. "Great dad," he said. "Lousy husband."

TWO

WHENEVER BUDDY HAD SOMETHING PRESSING ON HIS mind, he went to Central Park and ate a hot dog. Lately, he'd spent a lot of time in Central Park and a lot of money on hot dogs.

He found an empty bench facing the Transverse Road, sat down, unwrapped his hot dog, and took a bite. It was a lovely day in the park. A lovely day for getting your thoughts together and trying to figure out why your life felt so meaningless.

Buddy's concentration, however, was diverted by something going on nearby.

A small boy—five or six years old—was standing nearby observing a small gray squirrel that had attached itself to the side of a maple tree. Both the boy and the squirrel were perfectly still—neither moved. Buddy watched them with growing interest.

Finally, the squirrel scampered down the side of the tree and bounded along the pavement, coming to a sudden stop a few feet away from Buddy. Stealthily, the boy crept over and slid onto the bench beside Buddy. The two of them exchanged conspirators' smiles, then went back to watching the frozen squirrel.

Buddy tore a small piece of bun from his hot dog and gave it a toss. The squirrel pounced on the bread and gobbled it down. Then, it stood up on its hind legs and begged for more.

The boy was delighted. "Give it more," he urged Buddy enthusiastically.

"Okey doke." Buddy tore off another piece and gave it a toss.

He tossed it too far.

The bread landed right in the middle of the busy Transverse Road. The squirrel bounded after it and was instantly flattened by a passing taxi.

Buddy's stomach did a flipflop, and his face fell. He turned to the little boy. The kid gave him a dirty look and punched him hard in the arm. Then he ran off crying.

Buddy dumped the rest of his hot dog behind the bench and walked off in the opposite direction as quickly as his feet would carry him.

The dead squirrel was definitely a bad omen. Buddy decided to search for a good one. He made up his mind to try the zoo—he hadn't been there in years. As a matter of fact, the last time he'd been there had been with Marilyn. He hadn't thought of his ex-wife in a long time.

Marilyn.

They'd often come here to the park. Had often strolled the very path that Buddy was walking at this moment. That was the trouble with living your entire life in the same city. You were always running into some ghost of yourself coming around the next corner.

Marilyn didn't want children, Buddy thought to himself. That more than anything else had been the major contributing factor to their bust-up nearly twenty years ago. The marriage lasted barely six months, and afterwards Buddy swore that he'd never do it again. Marilyn, on the other hand, had remarried at least half a dozen times since. She was living in Wyoming or some place like that now. He'd lost touch.

Marilyn didn't want children. He said it over again in his mind.

Since the break-up, Buddy had concentrated his energies on two things—work and women. But there had been a time, more than twenty years ago, when he'd wanted a son. Was that it? Was that what was overwhelming him with discontent lately? Had that old longing returned now after all this time?

"Dad!" a small voice suddenly cried out from behind him.

Buddy turned instinctively, surprising himself, not to mention the small boy standing on the rise of the hill a few yards away.

It was apparent from the kid's disappointed face that he had mistaken Buddy for his father. Buddy's face looked disappointed, too.

Sheepishly, the boy turned and ran off. Buddy was overcome with an intense longing. He longed not to be mistaken for some boy's father—he longed to be one himself.

In that instant as he turned away and entered the zoo grounds, Buddy made up his mind to become one.

For the moment, though, he felt as if he needed to be around some children, and the zoo afforded him the perfect opportunity.

Buddy slipped into one of the lecture rooms and took a seat near the back. The room was full of children and mothers listening attentively to a pretty zoo guide who was narrating while a series of bird slides were projected onto a large screen.

There was something instantly familiar about the room. Buddy could've sworn he'd been there before. Many times, in fact.

He *had* been there before. It all came back to him. He'd been there on field trips as a kid over thirty years ago with his classmates and teachers. The room brought back warm memories of childhood.

Buddy looked around at the kids. It made him a little sad to think that they, too, would grow up and probably put this place out of their minds.

"The large emu," the guide was saying, "is one of the strangest birds of all."

Buddy studied the projection. He agreed. The emu certainly *looked* strange.

"The female emu does a very funny thing. After she lays her eggs, she leaves, letting the father emu raise the offspring all by himself."

"Really?"

The entire audience of mothers and children turned around in their seats and stared at Buddy. He sank down low with embarrassment. He hadn't meant to speak, the word had just jumped out of his mouth.

"And some birds," the guide continued, "are even more shifty than that. Some mommy birds will find a nest, throw out all the other eggs, and lay their own eggs for the unsuspecting mother to hatch and raise. Does anyone know what we call this kind of mother?"

"Smart!" said a woman near Buddy.

"No," said the guide, "we call this kind of mother a surrogate mother."

Buddy sat upright. Surrogate mother? The words danced around inside his brain. A nerve had been plucked.

Of course. It was just that simple. Why hadn't he thought of this before? A surrogate mother. Buddy exploded from his seat and tore out of the lecture room like a man possessed. Which is exactly what he was.

Buddy left the park at a fast trot and stole a cab from an elderly couple.

"Fifth and Eighty-fifth," he told the cabbie as they pulled into the traffic. Buddy settled back and smiled, more excited than he'd been in a long time. He had to get home and spring the idea on Celia. Celia was the perfect reverse barometer for such a scheme. If she hated it, Buddy could be sure it was a good idea.

As he rode toward home, Buddy tried not to remind himself that his longest running relationship with a woman was with his black middle-aged housekeeper.

Celia Woodman, however, did not think of herself as Buddy's housekeeper. She thought of herself as his keeper—period. Their relationship had been one drawn-out, never-ending battle. They fought and disagreed over practically everything under the sun. The woman, Buddy said time and time again, was impossible. But in twelve years time, it had never occurred to Celia to quit, nor had it ever crossed Buddy's mind to fire her. Though neither was likely to admit it, except perhaps under threat of torture, they genuinely *liked* each other.

They say you can tell a lot about a man from his home. Buddy's apartment on the Upper East Side of Manhattan was no exception to this adage.

Upon entering, one stared down a long entrance hall lined with framed photographs of countless sports figures and celebrities. The entrance hall gave way to an intimate sunken living room, the main purpose of which appeared to be to provide a proper setting for seduction. It was greatly aided by a large functional fireplace and an immense picture window that gave a magnificent (and at night, a quite romantic) view of Central Park and the lights beyond. Just down the hall, Buddy's bedroom carried along a similar motif since it generally served as the logical extension of the activities that began in the living room. Aside from two full bathrooms, there were also a kitchen (Celia's domain), a dining room (also Celia's domain), and a guest room (Celia's headquarters when there wasn't a visitor staying over, which was most of the time).

The most interesting room, however, was Buddy's den, situated at the end of the hall.

Few were allowed through its door, for this room was Buddy's only true refuge, his fortress of solitude. Even Celia was banned from its confines, and as a result it was always a mess.

The den was like some kind of shrine to the past. On its walls hung a variety of yellowing photographs of Buddy from his high school and college days. Most of these depicted Buddy in action—Buddy on the gridiron, Buddy on the baseball diamond, Buddy on the basketball court. There were also framed newspaper clippings, most of them now close to disintegration with age, all of them attesting to the achievements of a young athlete named Nelson "Buddy" Evans. This was a vulnerable room. There was something about it that gave one the impression of dreams unfulfilled.

Celia was defrosting the refrigerator when Buddy burst through the kitchen door. He looked like the cat that had swallowed the canary.

Celia had seen this look many times. She knew he was getting ready to drop a bomb on her. "All right," she said wearily, psychologically girding her loins for the combat ahead. "I don't know what you got on that thing you call a brain, but let's have it."

Buddy folded his arms across his chest and leaned against the sink. "I've decided I need a son," he stated matter-of-factly. "I'm going to be a father."

Celia just shrugged and went back to her work.

"What's wrong with that?" Buddy demanded.

"Who you gonna get to play mother in this little comedy?" Celia wanted to know.

"I can get anybody I want. I'm the most eligible bachelor in town."

Celia frowned. "Ain't nobody gonna stay married to you," she said. "You might be the most eligible bachelor in town, but a woman wouldn't last a day married to a man like you."

She turned her back on him and reached into the open freezer for an ice-cube tray. "No," she insisted, "ain't nobody gonna marry *you*."

Buddy smiled. He had her now. "I'm not going to get married," he stated matter-of-factly. "I'm going to hire a surrogate mother and raise the kid myself."

Celia faltered. The ice tray she was clutching fell out of her hand and hit the floor with a crash. Ice cubes clattered noisily about her feet.

"Like the emu," Buddy added.

Celia spun around and regarded him. Her face was stiff with anger. Buddy had successfully landed the first punch, and she didn't like it one bit.

"Well?" Buddy asked. "Don't you have anything to say?"

"I got plenty to say." Celia bent down and began collecting ice cubes. Buddy kneeled, too. In his victory he felt he could afford the gesture. "Mr. Evans," she sighed, "you'll never find a woman crazy enough to go along with that. You're the original Mr. Perfect. Pencil goes here, books go there, socks on the right, underwear on the left. You'd never find a woman could live up to your standards."

Buddy could feel his triumph slipping away. She was making perfect sense, goddamn her.

"I'm not talking about socks and underwear," Buddy protested as he helped her collect cubes. "I'm talking about a son. My son. Celia, listen to me. My life is a joke. It's empty. I have no roots."

"Okay, okay," she nodded, then fixed him with a look. "I'm gonna tell you exactly why it can't work."

"Okay. Tell me."

Celia paused for a moment, then let him have it. "Because, Mr. Evans, you're a cold fish."

"A cold fish?" Buddy sputtered. "What are you talking about? I *love* kids!"

"Sure. Somebody else's. Who don't?" Celia stood up and dumped a handful of ice cubes into the sink.

Buddy remained on the floor unaware that the ice around him was melting fast and soaking the knees of his trousers. "*You* have a family," he pointed out. He could hear the desperation in his own voice. She could always reduce him to this level. "*You* have kids. Don't tell me you don't believe in traditional values. I know for a dead solid fact that you believe in children."

"Depends how horny I am."

Buddy struggled to his feet, totally exasperated. "Celia," he proclaimed, "you're impossible."

"And you're a cold fish."

Buddy sighed and dropped himself limply into one of the kitchen chairs.

Celia went back to work on the refrigerator, humming happily. She'd won. She always won.

"I'm not a cold fish," Buddy protested weakly. "I have inner warmth."

Celia looked at him and smiled. "You also got wet knees," she pointed out.

THREE

PEOPLE ALWAYS DESCRIBED MAGGIE HARDEN AS "A striking young lady," the kind of woman who riveted attention wherever she went. For this reason, Maggie tended to downplay her good looks whenever she could. She rarely wore make-up and preferred to dress informally in jeans and loose sweaters. Besides, they were all she could afford on the meager allowance she alloted herself. Maggie had decided long ago to get by on talent alone. Taking this route, she found that the going was tough. She'd been in New York for two years now, studying cello at Juilliard, waitressing at Woodson's, and giving lessons on the side whenever she could. The word "relaxation" was hardly in her vocabulary. She hadn't been to a movie or play in all the time she'd been in Manhattan. She'd never even been to Central Park even though it was only a few blocks away.

Men pestered her endlessly for dates. Aside from being quite pretty, Maggie had been born with the misfortune (in *her* opinion) of having the most incredible brown eyes people had ever seen. Whenever she could, she wore dark glasses.

Her one-room apartment in a crumbling building in the West Seventies reflected her life—all messed up. The place, which was barely big enough to cram a bed and a dresser into, looked like somebody's sick idea of an ad for leisure living on the San Andreas fault line. The rug—if there indeed was a rug—was indiscernible beneath a sea of ancient sheet music. Any burglar who broke in would figure somebody had beat him to it and leave. Not that Maggie had anything of great value— unless there was a sudden world shortage of waste paper. She didn't even have a TV.

What Maggie did have was *hope*. The hope that her hard work and self-denial—not to mention her talent— would one day take her out of this place and magically whisk her away to a beautiful land of fantasy called Paris. Her heart was set on it. Several months earlier, she'd applied to the École de Musique in Paris, hoping she was at last worthy of studying cello with the great Renais himself.

She waited with trepidation for the reply.

Then, one lovely blue-skyed day, the letter arrived.

Maggie had always been especially proud of her ability to remain strong in the face of adversity. Never once in all her twenty-six years had she been afraid to open a letter.

Up until now.

Standing in the middle of her cramped room, Maggie held the crisp white envelope at arm's length and attempted to divine some kind of psychic clue as to its contents. No dice. She was only aware of the fact that her hand had begun to shake and that the letter was fluttering like a leaf in a windstorm.

Why couldn't she open it? There was a very good reason. The contents of the letter she clutched in her hand would decide for Maggie whether her life had been in vain or if it was just beginning. How much courage did it take to open a small white envelope postmarked Paris?

Take it to work and let *Cathy* open it. She was nosey, she'd love to do it, Maggie reasoned. Plus that way there'd be somebody present to share the good news. (And somebody present to prevent her from putting her head in the oven if the news was—God forbid! —bad.)

Maggie placed the letter on the kitchen table and changed into her waitress uniform. While zipping up the back, she caught sight of her frightened face in the closet mirror and forced a hopeful smile. If the letter contained good news, her waitressing days would be numbered. But if it contained bad news . . . no! It *had* to be good news.

Maggie shoved the letter into her pocket and ran the whole way to Woodson's Coffee Shop.

Cathy Kramer, in *her* waitress uniform, was perched on a stool in Woodson's kitchen, chewing a cuticle and waiting for the shift to begin, when the back door flew open and Maggie rushed in. Without a word of greeting, Maggie thrust the letter into Cathy's hand.

Cathy saw the postmark, and her eyes grew bigger. Then a look of fear swept her face. "No, Maggie," she said and handed the letter back. "It's your letter. You open it."

Maggie stared at the envelope, now crinkled and bent. She felt like crying. She'd never been so scared of anything in her entire life.

"Maggie," Cathy urged, "open the letter."

"Oh, shit!" Maggie grabbed an electric carving knife from the counter, switched it on, and sliced open the envelope with one deft stroke. She looked at Cathy with genuine terror in her eyes. "I'm so afraid to look," she confessed.

"Open it, Mag," Cathy prodded, trying to keep the valve shut on her own excitement. "Get it over with."

Maggie took a deep breath and unfolded the single sheet of paper. She scanned it quickly.

"Well?" Cathy asked, unable to disguise the tension in her own voice. "Don't keep me in suspense."

Maggie looked up from the page and smiled. The smile grew bigger. And bigger.

"You got it?"

"I got it!" Maggie screamed.

"You got it!" Cathy jumped off her stool and wrapped her arms around Maggie. The two of them hopped around Woodson's kitchen like a couple of happy schoolgirls.

"Oh, Maggie," Cathy was filled with excitement, "you're going to Paris. Paris, France!"

Maggie flopped down on the vacated stool. Her heart was beating doubly quick. "And not only that," she said, "but I'll be studying with Renais. He's absolutely the best there is." She could feel tears beginning to form in her eyes. "They *want* me."

"I'm so happy for you," Cathy bubbled.

"It's Renais's last year." Maggie clasped the letter to her breast. "Oh God, Cathy, I've worked so hard for this." Carefully, she read the letter over again. "It says I've got to tell them by the end of the month whether I'm coming or not."

Cathy regarded her with confusion. "What do you mean whether you're coming or not. Of course you're coming."

"It's gonna cost a whole lot of money," Maggie pointed out. "A lot more than the tips I make *here*."

"But you've got a whole year to earn it. Didn't you say it wouldn't be beginning till next year?"

"Yeah," Maggie nodded, her brow furrowing. "I'll have to give lessons every spare minute, but even then . . ."

"Don't worry, you're gonna do it," Cathy assured her. She hadn't been president of her high school pep club for nothing. "I know you, kiddo. You'll find a way to get the money."

The smile returned to Maggie's face. "Paris," she sighed. "I'm going to Paris."

The manager's dark shadow fell over them.

"*Pardon moi, mademoiselle,*" he croaked, "but we got customers out there. You wanna move your asses?"

They moved their asses.

FOUR

"PROBLEMS," KURT SAID, DUMPING ABOUT HALF OF THE sugar container into his coffee cup. Buddy's mad schemes could make him forsake his diet faster than anything else. "I see nothing but problems."

He and Buddy were encamped in their usual booth at Woodson's.

"That's why I'm telling this to you," Buddy explained patiently. "So we can *avoid* the problems. You're a lawyer, you'll find a way."

"Listen," Kurt said confidentially, "I happen to think the whole thing is immoral."

"Since when has that stopped you?"

"Why don't you just adopt a kid for crying out loud?"

"It's not the same thing. I want a kid that's *me*. My flesh and blood. To carry on the line. I'm serious about this, Kurt."

Kurt stared out the window for a long moment. Then he turned back and frowned. "It's insane," he said.

"It's *not* insane," Buddy argued. "Just draw me up a contract. I want it all spelled out up front. And I don't want just anybody for the mother. She's got to be the right size, the right temperature. Nothing weird about her."

"And who's going to find this mystery mother?"

"*We* are," Buddy answered with a grin.

Kurt rubbed his face and went back to looking out the window. He knew that when Buddy got an idea into his head, it was impossible to sway him.

"I'm going to ask some of the ladies I know," Buddy explained. "Meantime, I want you to check out the pros."

"The *pros*?" Kurt looked at him in surprise. "What do you mean 'the *pros*'?"

"There are women who do this all the time."

"I don't believe you."

"They're all over the place. Don't you ever watch Phil Donahue?"

Kurt shook his head and felt like ordering a dozen glazed doughnuts. "No woman in her right mind would do what you want her to do."

"Aha," Buddy said with a smile, "that's where you're wrong." He grinned confidently. "I'll bet you most of the single women in this very restaurant would go along with it."

"All right, smart guy." Kurt accepted the challenge and caught Maggie's attention at a nearby table. He waved her over. "Let's just find out about that. We'll ask the waitress. Waitresses are notoriously single."

Maggie arrived with the coffee pot and a smile. Smiles sometimes earned decent tips, and Maggie had one hell of a nice smile. "More coffee, gentlemen?" she asked politely.

"We're having a little argument," Kurt told her, "and I wonder if you'd mind joining in for a second."

"I'm not supposed to," Maggie replied, still smiling sweetly. These male customers were always finding some excuse to take up her time. Horny bastards.

"It's okay," Kurt assured her. "The manager is a good friend of ours." He slid over and made room for her in the booth.

"Well, all right," Maggie agreed, sitting down with some reluctance. "But it'll have to be quick, gentlemen. I've got a bunch of orders backing up."

34

"It'll just take a second," Kurt promised. "We just need a female opinion."

Maggie grimaced. Male customers were *always* wanting a female opinion.

"Please hear us out," Buddy implored, giving her his most winning and sincere smile. "It's important."

The smile seemed to work. Maggie nodded for Kurt to continue.

"I warn you, it's gonna sound a little weird, but please bear with me," Kurt said. "Okay. A friend of ours wants to have a son—"

"A *distant* friend," Buddy interjected.

"But the thing is, he doesn't want to get married."

"Is he gay?" Maggie asked.

"Of course not!" Buddy snapped.

"The question is," Kurt went on, "do you feel, as a woman, that you would bear a child for a man who was not your husband?"

Maggie thought about it for a few seconds, then shrugged indifferently. "Sure," she said. "If the price was right."

Buddy grinned triumphantly.

"But I think the opposite should be true as well," Maggie continued. "A man should be willing to help out a lady who doesn't want a husband."

"You're a very rational young lady," Buddy complimented her. "And a good waitress, too."

"May I go now?" she asked.

"Of course," Buddy replied. "And thank you."

Maggie got up and hurried to the kitchen where her orders were piling up. Buddy beamed at Kurt. Kurt once again turned away and stared morosely out the window.

"*Now* what do you think?" Buddy asked.

"I *still* see problems," Kurt muttered.

FIVE

MAGGIE WAS ON A PARTIAL SCHOLARSHIP AT JUILLIARD
School of Music. This place was where the great
musicians came from. The real class acts. Juilliard symbolized refinement and perfection. And right now for
Maggie, it symbolized poverty. Students don't make
much money. Music students make even less. But at
least they've got a skill. Maggie had her cello. And she
had Smog. Not the pollution problem. The punk rock
band called Smog.

Smog played all the dingy, grimy clubs on the Lower
East Side, and when they got a name for themselves
among the "in" punk crowd, they moved up. To the
dingy, grimy clubs on the Upper West Side. But it was a
way to make a few bucks on the weekends, and even
though it wasn't the kind of music she'd always
dreamed of playing, what the hell? It paid the rent. Or
part of it.

The evening after Maggie got her good news from
Paris, she left the coffee shop and raced over to Billy's apartment. Billy was another Juilliard student who
played the oboe. He wasn't exactly crazy about playing
with Smog, but he did it for the cash, too. Besides, he
got a kick out of it. More than Maggie did. And it was
their constant arguments over the group, how it should

be run and how "big" they should try to become, that forced Maggie to move out of their shared apartment and go to a place of her own. They were still friends and occasionally something more, but their relationship was now at that "neither here nor there" position. Billy always said they'd never work.

"Everybody knows that woodwinds and strings make for lousy relationships," he'd always remind her.

"I'm glad nobody told that to Vivaldi."

At least they could laugh about it.

But Maggie wasn't so sure about Billy's and the rest of Smog's reactions to the news that she had been accepted to study in Paris and, if it were possible, would leave the next morning. Of course that wasn't possible, but it was likely that she'd have to leave the band for a more lucrative job, and that they might not like.

Billy's apartment was where the band practiced. It was one of those loft places in Soho. One huge room where you did everything. Almost. Like the one-room schoolhouses you see in westerns.

But it had space and sunlight, two things that came at a premium in New York. And it also had no neighbors, which considering the din that Smog put out, was a blessing. After the group began to rehearse, even the winos moved out. In fact after the group began, Maggie noticed that even the roaches had disappeared.

That special "din" was what she heard going up in the elevator. Naturally it was a freight elevator, which as Billy always pointed out was actually larger than her apartment. Ha, ha, ha.

"I'm not moving back, Billy."

When she got off at the third floor, she was greeted by the group's newest song, "I Was a Teenage Wino."

The two other members of the band besides she and Billy were not Juilliard students. It was hard to say exactly *what* they were. Whatever, the "Three Bs" did not mean Bach, Beethoven, and Brahms to them. It might have meant bass, bass, and more bass. Johnnie

PATERNITY

Sonnet, self-proclaimed poet of the punk generation, and Phones Labone, his lady friend who constantly wore headphones, made up band members three and four.

They were a cute couple—Johnnie with his skin-tight black pants and white socks, and Phones with her purple hair and omnipresent headphones. She had several pairs, much like a proper lady has gloves. Phones had a set for informal times such as morning and noon and a set for formal affairs at night. She also had a few other sets of phones for very special occasions. Like her white ones for weddings.

Maggie was late for the rehearsal so she tried to enter inconspicuously. A very hard thing to do in a forty- by sixty-foot room with no furniture in it.

The band stopped playing.

"Where've you been, Maggie?" asked Billy.

"You're late, sweetheart," said Johnnie.

"Wow," said Phones.

Better get right to the point, thought Maggie.

"I gotta talk to you guys."

"You missed two rehearsals this week already," said Billy.

"I know, I know. I've been working."

Johnnie put his arm around Phones and sauntered towards Maggie.

"Our record came out this morning."

Maggie didn't seem to hear him. "Great."

Billy made his way to the kitchen area and opened the refrigerator. Maggie followed.

"Billy, I gotta talk to you," she said.

"Didn't you hear what Johnnie just said?"

"I heard him," Maggie said quickly, "but something else's come up."

Billy was taking out the makings for a tuna fish sandwich. He put a milk carton on the counter. Maggie, out of habit, picked it up, smelled it, and quickly put it back down.

"You don't throw that milk out soon and you're gonna have to baptize it."

Johnnie and Phones came closer.

"Did you hear what I said about our record?"

"I heard."

"Well, aren't you happy?" asked Johnnie, looking quite hurt by Maggie's nonchalance.

"I'm happy. I really am." Maggie saw that it meant a lot to him. She smiled and kissed him. "Congratulations."

Meanwhile, Billy had taken a large piece of folded tin foil from the refrigerator and laid it on the counter.

"What's in that," Maggie asked with a suspicious leer at the crinkly lump.

"I forget," said Billy. "Anybody remember what's in this tin foil here?"

Johnnie shook his head. Phones was lost in a song.

"Just throw it out," suggested Maggie.

"It might be valuable," Billy said as he raised a fork and aimed it at the lump as if some creature from a 1950s horror movie was going to come crawling out. Maggie slowly tore the tin foil apart, using two spatulas. Johnnie took a few steps back.

Maggie managed to open the foil.

Inside was a wristwatch.

"Damn. That's where I put it!" Phones yelled as she grabbed the watch and put it on her wrist. "Whew, that's a cold sucker."

She and Johnnie walked back to their instruments and warmed up. Maggie spoke in low tones to Billy. Then she realized that even if she screamed, he would just about be able to hear her over the music.

"I got the letter from France today!"

"What?" Billy screamed back.

"I said I heard from Renais!"

"Yeah. Nice day."

Maggie was about to give up when the music suddenly stopped.

"Let's go see if they got our record on the racks yet," said Johnnie as Billy put the finishing touches on his sandwich.

"We can talk on the way," Billy said to Maggie.

On the way to the record store through the dark streets, Phones kept staring at Billy. Maggie wanted to talk to him alone, but that looked like it wasn't going to happen.

"Hey, man, that isn't tuna fish, is it?" asked Phones.

Billy shot a look at Maggie.

"No," he said, turning back to Phones.

"Good," continued Phones, " 'cause the tuna fishers are killing off the porpoises. They cast their huge nets over the water and that keeps the porpoises from being able to come up and breathe. They drown in the water."

Maggie nodded. "Heavy."

"You sure that's not tuna fish?" asked Phones.

"No," said Billy. "It's porpoise."

"That's cool," declared Phones as she drifted off into the world of her headsets.

Maggie quickly took the chance to tell Billy.

"I got accepted to the school in Paris."

Billy stopped dead in his tracks. Phones and Johnnie disappeared into the record store.

Maggie looked at Billy. "I got accepted. Did you hear me? To study with Renais. In Paris."

Billy just stood there. Then a smile crept onto his face. Before long it was ear to ear. He grabbed Maggie and picked her up off the ground.

"That's great! That's wonderful! Oh God, Maggie! I'm so damned happy for you!"

"I know. Thanks. But I gotta quit the band."

Billy wasn't listening. He just kept laughing and hugging her.

"Did you hear me?" Maggie repeated. "I gotta quit the band."

This time he heard her. His smile died.

"You have to quit the band?"

"I need a lot of money."

"Maybe the record will do well."

"Oh, come on, Billy, we both know how the record's gonna do. It'll sell a hundred copies here and in Pittsburgh, and then it'll die."

Billy walked into the store. Johnnie was arguing with the clerk.

"What do you mean you never heard of Smog? I'm Johnnie Sonnet, and I'm telling you you better hear of it because it's the next smash of the season, pal."

Johnnie slammed his fist on the counter, causing the clerk's sandwich to jump six inches. As he and Phones stormed out of the store, Phones shot a sharp look at the sandwich.

"That's not tuna fish, is it?"

Phones and Johnnie walked quickly up the street.

"You gonna tell them you're gonna quit the band?" Billy asked Maggie.

"I guess I have to."

But she didn't. She didn't say anything about this new "job" to them, and she kept playing with them for their next few gigs. She needed the money.

SIX

AND SO BEGAN THE GREAT SURROGATE MOTHER HUNT. Buddy got out his little black book and began putting check marks beside the names of the women he felt would be likely to go along with such a stunt. He only came up with three.

The first one turned out to be in Jamaica on her honeymoon. The second told him to go to hell. And the third . . . the third agreed to meet him. Buddy made sure not to tell her what it was all about, only that it was a matter of life and death.

Buddy sat in the Oak Bar, sipping a Scotch and water and thinking to himself. It would be nice to see Janice again. How long had it been since the last time? Nearly three years, he figured. Janice Penzler with the big . . .

Yes, Buddy assured himself, it would be nice to see her again.

"Buddy?" Janice's voice was unmistakable. "Buddy Evans?"

Buddy looked up from his Scotch and nearly heaved. Nuns had always had that effect on him.

"J-J-Janice?" he managed.

Janice adjusted her habit and slipped onto the stool beside him. "Hello, Buddy," she said pleasantly. "Now what's this about life and death?"

43

Kurt had been right, the bastard. There were going to be problems.

One of the problems was named Miss Werner.

"Miss who?"

"Miss Werner," Kurt explained on the other end of the line.

Buddy sat back in the chair behind his desk and watched dozens of workmen in the arena below, setting up for the circus.

"I hope this one hasn't taken her vows yet. Damn, I was so embarrassed I bought 200 tickets to her church raffle."

"You'll like Miss Werner, Buddy. She's done this kind of thing before."

"How many times before?"

"A couple."

Buddy frowned. "I want a surrogate mother. Not a Xerox machine."

"Just give her a chance, Buddy."

"I will, I will. I think I know what I've been doing wrong so far. I've been too aggressive. Too on the money. I'll just be more casual about this lady."

"Good. And I hope it works because I'm a lawyer, not a pimp, buster."

"Right."

Buddy hung up and pressed the intercom button.

"Send in Miss Werner."

He stood up and adjusted his tie and his smile. Miss Werner walked through the door. She was pleasant-looking enough. Not beautiful but somehow "medium."

Buddy held out his hand. "Hi, I'm Buddy Evans."

"I know," Miss Werner said, smiling. "I'm Janice Werner."

"Won't you sit down?"

"Thank you."

So far so good.

"Coffee?"

"No, thank you."

Buddy took a quick inventory. Nothing seemed "wrong" with her. He sat down behind the desk and picked up the book of children's names he'd been browsing through all morning.

"Quinby," he said. "It's a boy's name. What do you think of it?"

Miss Werner smiled. Buddy smiled. It was a good way to break the ice.

"It sucks."

The ice was not only broken, but it was melting fast. Buddy stared at her.

"I beg your pardon?"

"I said it sucks."

"I thought that's what you said." But it wasn't what she said that bothered him so much as what she said it with. Because for the first time, Buddy realized that her teeth were not the only things in her mouth. Braces stared out at him, too.

"What are those, Miss Werner?"

"What are what?"

"On your teeth."

"They're braces."

Buddy nodded. "I know they're braces, but do you have to wear them?"

"No, actually they're the latest in costume jewelry." She smirked. "Of course I have to wear them."

Down in the arena below, someone sounded a horn. The noise drifted into Buddy's office like the charge signal for a cavalry battle. It was not inappropriate.

"Well, Miss Werner, I don't know if I want my son to have a smile like the Fifty-ninth Street Bridge."

She smiled politely. "Well, Mr. Evans, he could have your forehead."

"What's wrong with my forehead?"

"Look at those lines. It appears to be suffering from erosion."

"That's very amusing. However, if we're going to discuss appearances, I might add that your nose isn't exactly what one would call classic."

Miss Werner stood up and faced him, nose to unclassical nose, across the desk.

"Has anyone ever suggested that you plant corn in your eyebrows, Mr. Evans?"

"What's wrong with my eyebrows?"

"Nothing . . . if you're into wildlife."

Buddy's face fell. He stared across his desk at this witch. His face lit up as he focused in on her hair.

"While we're on the subject of hair, Miss Werner, we might discuss the *mat* on the top of your head."

"What about it?"

"Do you shampoo or do you crop dust?"

The rest of the meeting was just about as friendly. Fortunately, it didn't last very long. Just long enough for Miss Werner to storm out of the room and slam the door behind her as she left.

"What the hell did you say to her?" Kurt was upset.

"I don't know what she got so excited about. I mean I just mentioned some physical factors, and she went nuts. I don't want anyone like that to have my son."

"What about that Emily lady?" Kurt decided it was best to change the subject.

Buddy winced. Emily was another old girlfriend he thought would be perfect. He invited her out, and they had a lovely evening together. They dined. They ate. They laughed. They walked home together in the rain. Buddy remembered the part about the rain the best because it reminded him of the umbrella. The umbrella that Emily kept hitting him with over and over again just after he asked her to be the surrogate mother of his son. It was a cheap umbrella. What the hell?

Laura Loftus stepped off the elevator and strode purposefully down the carpeted corridor towards

Buddy Evans's office. When Buddy's secretary had called and asked if she would be interested in redecorating part of her boss's apartment—a nursery, to be precise—Laura had jumped at the opportunity. She knew that Buddy Evans was an important man in New York. An important man with important friends. *Rich, important friends.* This was her chance to move her struggling interior decorating service into the big time. She looked forward to meeting Buddy Evans and was determined to get the job at all costs.

As she entered the outer office, Laura collided with Iris the secretary who was on her way out.

"Who are you?" Iris demanded, moving past Laura and pausing momentarily in the doorway for her reply.

"I'm Laura Loftus. The decorator."

"Right, right. We spoke on the phone."

"I realize I don't have an appointment, but I was in the neighborhood and took a chance that Mr. Evans might have some free time—"

"Right, right. Go on in. He's not busy." And with that, Iris was out the door and on her way to lunch.

Sitting in his office, Buddy poured two fingers of Scotch into a tumbler and drank it down in one gulp. The Great Surrogate Mother Hunt was not going well. Already today he'd interviewed a dozen more losers Kurt had dug up. He suspected that Kurt was doing it on purpose, finding the worst types imaginable in order to dissuade Buddy from carrying out his scheme.

Buddy checked the note pad on his desk. The next interviewee was somebody named Jenny Diablo. *Jenny Diablo?* What kind of a name was that? He could just imagine her. Probably rode with the Hell's Angels.

"Mr. Evans?"

Buddy looked up and saw the most beautiful woman he'd laid eyes on in weeks, standing in his doorway. For nearly an entire fifteen seconds, he just stood there, gaping. Jenny Diablo, he thought to himself. Why, she's nothing at *all* like her name. She's composed, well-dressed . . . and absolutely beautiful.

"Mr. Evans?" Laura Loftus repeated, growing more uncomfortable by the second. She was used to having men stare at her, but this guy was like one of those wolves in the cartoons whose tongue hangs down to the floor.

"I'm sorry," Buddy apologized, blinking his eyes several times and returning to reality. "Please come in and have a seat."

She was perfect!

Laura came into the room and sat down in the leather chair across from the desk. Without once taking his eyes from her, Buddy came from behind the desk and began to walk around her in a slow circle, allowing no little detail of her physiognomy to escape his attention. If she had any flaws, they were well-hidden.

Much impressed, Buddy returned to his chair behind the desk. "Well, well, well," he said with a strange, fascinated look in his eyes. "Well, well, well."

Laura noticed the diploma hanging on the wall behind him. "I see you went to Fordham," she observed nervously. "I went to Columbia."

"Really?" He was barely listening. "I think that's just wonderful."

Laura shifted uncomfortably in her chair. "Mr. Evans," she said, "do you know why I'm here?"

Buddy leaned forward and rested his elbows on the desk top. "I know exactly why you're here."

"Good," Laura breathed a sigh of relief. "Then why don't we get started?"

"Quinby," said Buddy.

"Excuse me?"

"Quinby."

Laura hadn't the slightest idea of what he was talking about. Better fake it, though. "No thanks," she said uneasily. "I just had lunch."

"No, no," Buddy corrected. "Quinby is a boy's name."

"Oh."

"It's Scandinavian and means 'from the womb of a woman.'"

Laura nodded. She was beginning to wonder if perhaps this man was insane. Maybe he'd murdered the real Buddy Evans and assumed his identity.

Buddy figured it was time to get down to business. "Just for the record," he said, "I want to assure you that absolutely nothing sexual will enter into our relationship."

Laura's eyes opened wide.

"I mean," continued Buddy, staring at this very attractive woman in front of him, "that some men would expect entanglements." He waved a hand in the air as he searched for a better word. "Oh, what the hell? They'd expect emotional and sexual involvement. I just want you to know that this is a business transaction and that's the name of the game. Business."

Laura was glad that he had explained. Here was a man who wanted to spell out, up front, the rules. She liked that. Men were always hitting on her and it was beginning to make her think about taking on any more men clients. "I'm glad you said that, Mr. Evans, and I couldn't agree more. Purely business."

"Purely business," repeated Buddy. "You're performing a service and I'm paying for it. Cut and dried."

"Cut and dried is how I like it."

"That's how it's going to be." Buddy stared at her as she visibly relaxed in the chair. "May I see your breasts?"

Laura sat up. "What?"

Buddy didn't change expressions. "Part of the deal. After all they're like tools of the trade, right? What I mean is when you look at my—oh, what the hell—at my genitals, don't think of them as genitals. Think of

them as, say, a potato peeler. Or an electric blender."
Laura stood up. She didn't pray often, but here was a
case where prayer was needed. Buddy continued.
"Whatever you do, just don't think of my organs as
sexual. They're tools, not genitals."

That did it. Without another moment's hesitation,
Laura turned and ran out of the office just as fast as
her feet would carry her.

Buddy stood up, looking perplexed. "Jenny?" he
called after her. "What's the matter?"

He couldn't understand. Had he said something out
of line? The only thing he knew for sure was that this
woman was absolutely perfect, and he couldn't afford
to let her get away. Buddy grabbed his coat and gave
chase.

Laura wisely rejected the elevator and took the stairs
instead. The sooner she got out of there the better.
Forget about a high-class clientele, she told herself.
They were probably all a bunch of perverts like this
Buddy Evans character.

Buddy made the mistake of taking the elevator. Had
he taken the stairs, he might have caught her. By the
time he reached Eighth Avenue, it was too late. Just
down the block at the taxi stand, he spotted Laura
climbing into a cab.

But Buddy was determined to catch her. While her
cab pulled into the flow of traffic, he ran to the taxi
stand. Luckily there was one waiting. He yanked open
its back door and slid in just as someone was doing
likewise on the other side.

Buddy found a cello case thrust into his lap and a
young woman seated beside him. He did not recognize
her as the waitress from Woodson's.

"Excuse me," Maggie protested hotly. "This happens
to be *my* cab."

Buddy ignored her and shouted to the driver, point-
ing at Laura's taxi, "Follow that cab!"

The driver turned around to see what kind of nut he had sitting in his back seat.

"Corner of Bank and Hudson," Maggie instructed.

"Forget Bank and Hudson," Buddy yelled, pushing the cello case off his lap. "Follow that cab! I'll pay you fifty bucks over the meter!"

"Put your money where your mouth is," the cabbie replied.

"Hey, just a minute!" Maggie fumed. "That's not fair!"

Buddy pulled a wad of tens out of his pocket and pressed them up against the separation glass for the driver to see. In this cab, money talked. The cabbie pulled into traffic and started after Laura's cab.

"This is kidnapping!" Maggie shouted.

"Just take it easy," Buddy told her. "This is a matter of life and death."

Maggie was about to yell something in reply when she suddenly recognized him. "It's *you*," she gaped in bewilderment. "I should have *known* you were crazy about that baby business."

For the first time, Buddy took his eyes off Laura's cab and looked at the woman beside him. "I know you," he said. "You're a waitress at Woodson's."

"I'm not a waitress, I'm a musician." Maggie indicated the cello case in her lap. "And I'm late."

"Look," Buddy tried to reassure her, "I'm sorry, but I have to catch the woman in that taxi. It's very important."

"Well, it's very important that *I* be someplace, too. I had this cab first, you know."

"Don't worry." Buddy was barely listening to her protests. He cranked down his window and stuck his head out in order to keep Laura's cab in sight. "I'll see that you get to wherever it is that you're going."

The driver made a sudden right, and Buddy spilled back into the cab, sprawling across Maggie.

"You're on my cello," Maggie said, shoving him back into a sitting position.

Buddy looked at the cello case, clearly puzzled. "But I thought you were a waitress," he said.

"I only do that to stay alive," she answered coolly. "I happen to be a musician. And a darn good one, too, for your information. I'm almost a prodigy."

"You're too old to be a prodigy," Buddy told her. "Prodigies are kids. Like *my* kid. My kid is gonna be a prodigy."

The cab made a hard left, and this time Maggie fell against Buddy. "Who's in that cab anyway?" she demanded, trying to extricate herself.

"Jenny. Jenny Diablo."

"What'd she do? Steal something?"

"We had a little misunderstanding. I asked to see her breasts, and she ran away."

"Well," Maggie observed philosophically, "some women are funny that way."

After a nerve-jangling half-hour of sharp turns and narrow escapes through the streets of New York—not to mention setting the world's record for running red lights—the chase finally came to an end on a pier in lower Manhattan where Laura's cab screeched to a halt in front of a large tour boat that was taking on the last of its passengers.

Buddy was hopping up and down in his seat as they drew closer. "There she goes!" he yelled excitedly as Laura emerged from her cab and raced up the gangplank.

Buddy shoved a handful of cash through the driver's slot. "Don't spend it all in one place," he said as they came to a sudden stop.

"Anytime, Mac," the cabbie said gleefully and began to scoop up the money.

"Well," Maggie sighed with relief, "I'm glad that's over."

But it wasn't.

"Come on," Buddy insisted, grabbing her by the arm and pulling her out of the cab with him. She was barely able to keep her grip on her cello case.

"Wait a minute!" Maggie demanded as Buddy hauled her along the pier toward the gangplank. "Hey, I've still got a lesson to get to!"

Buddy caught a final glimpse of Laura joining the throng on deck. "Hurry up," Buddy shouted. "We can't let her get away!"

Maggie found herself caught in Buddy's slipstream as he clattered up the gangplank, dragging her along. "What am *I* coming along for?" Maggie wanted to know.

"Because you're a woman," Buddy answered. "I may need you to interpret for me. I can't afford to let her get away. She's absolutely perfect."

"Absolutely perfect for what?"

"For my son."

What was this guy, Maggie asked herself, some kind of pimp?

Within a few seconds they found themselves on the crowded open-air deck. Buddy looked around desperately. Surprisingly, the boat was full of old women. Everywhere you looked, old women. It looked as if every ladies' garden club in the United States was present.

"Wait a minute," Maggie said suspiciously, looking around at the ancient visages. "I think we just stepped into the Twilight Zone."

"She's here someplace," Buddy said emphatically.

"Well, one thing is for sure," Maggie remarked. "She shouldn't be too hard to spot. Not if she's under ninety."

"We'll find her," Buddy promised, "and when we do—"

His next few words were obliterated by the ship's whistle. Had Buddy happened to turn and look back at the pier, he would have noticed Laura Loftus slipping down the gangplank to safety. But Buddy did not look back. He was too busy scanning faces even to realize that the ship was pulling out.

Near the bow, the middle-aged tour guide picked up his megaphone, put a smile on his otherwise dour face, and went into his act. "Welcome, ladies and gentlemen, to the tour of a lifetime—glorious Manhattan Island!"

Maggie disengaged herself from Buddy and went angrily to the rail, struggling to keep hold of her cello case.

"What's the matter?" Buddy asked, coming over to join her. He put a foot on the bottom bar of the rail and boosted himself up in order to get a clear view over the white-haired heads of his fellow passengers.

"I'm gonna miss three lessons on account of you," Maggie sulked, watching the pier grow smaller in the distance. "And I happen to *need* that money."

"Don't sweat," Buddy said. "I'll pay you for your time. It's important that we find this woman."

"Okay, girls," the tour guide was saying, "we're gonna head north first, past the South Street Museum, and under the Brooklyn and Manhattan Bridges. But before that I want you to look real quick over your left shoulders—"

Obediently, the old women on board turned and looked over their left shoulders.

"—and you'll see Beth Israel Hospital. I had my gall bladder taken out there back in '62."

Buddy took Maggie by the arm and began moving through the dense crowd, trying to find Laura. His path was suddenly blocked by a formidable-looking little woman. Though she was on the far side of eighty, fire blazed in her beady little eyes. She was obviously the ringleader.

"What's the big idea crashing our excursion?" she demanded, poking Buddy's chest with a long, gnarled finger.

"We're looking for somebody," Buddy explained, putting on his best smile. "A young lady."

A small crowd of elderly women began to form around them, sensing a confrontation, perhaps even smelling blood in the air.

"That'll be twenty bucks," the ringleader asserted, holding out her hand palm up. "Twenty bucks apiece."

"I'm not here for the tour," Buddy said, beginning to feel hemmed in. "I'm just looking for somebody who got on board."

"Girls," the ringleader addressed her cronies, "we have a *crasher*."

A rumble of disapproval came from the rest of the gang. Buddy quickly dug out his wallet. "All right, all right," he said, giving in. "I'll pay. Only don't throw us overboard."

He thrust forty dollars into the old woman's greedy claw. Satisfied, she stepped aside to let Buddy and Maggie pass, her eyes sparkling with triumph. Maggie tried to hide a smile.

"Come on," Buddy took her by the arm, and they began to mingle with the rest of the passengers. "I hope she didn't sneak off or something."

"First on our left is the United Nations where they do all that world stuff," the guide's megaphoned voice followed them around the boat as they searched in vain for Laura. "But right before that, you'll notice, is Belle-vue Hospital. I had a herniated disc fixed there. Top-class doctors. Top-class. I had an Oriental. You get a herniated disc, go to an Oriental."

After a thorough search of the boat—Maggie came in handy checking out the ladies' room—Buddy and Maggie returned to the upper deck and flopped down on an empty bench. Buddy's face and body sagged with disappointment.

"I really wanted that woman," Buddy said quietly. "I wanted her to be the mother of my child."

"I guess she got off," Maggie said sympathetically. "Tough break."

Buddy nodded, feeling sorry for himself.

"You really love her, don't you?" Maggie asked, beginning to share his sense of loss.

"Love who?"

"The woman we're looking for."

"Jenny?" Buddy looked at Maggie in confusion. "How could I be in love with her? I just met her an hour ago."

Now it was Maggie's turn to look confused. "You just said you wanted her to be the mother of your child."

"My son. I wanted her to be the mother of my son."

"You mean you've already *got* a son?"

"No." Buddy shook his head, nearing exasperation. "I wanted to hire her to have a baby for me—a son. I don't want to get married. I think marriage stinks."

Maggie's jaw dropped as her mind flashed back to the argument in Woodson's. "But what do you want a son for?" she asked.

"For me. For the ages. For continuity. I'm forty-four years old and what have I got to leave behind that'll say Buddy Evans was here?"

Maggie could see that he meant it. She nodded sympathetically. "I can sorta see what you mean. I can understand wanting to have a kid."

"You can?"

"Well, as a woman. Having a kid is an important experience for a woman. It's something most women—including myself—want to go through some time in their lives."

"It's something *I'd* like to go through if I could," Buddy remarked. "But I can't. I need a woman."

"You want to raise the kid yourself?"

"That's the whole idea."

Maggie frowned. "I don't envy you for that. I wouldn't mind giving birth but, boy, I don't know about raising a kid myself. I don't think I could handle a thing like that. I've got a career to concentrate on."

Buddy felt an electric excitement growing inside him. A strange smile came over his face as he looked at Maggie, studying her with intense concentration.

Maggie could feel his eyes burning into her. She looked at him. "What's the matter?" she asked nervously.

"What's your name?" There was a quiver in his voice.

"Maggie."

Buddy swallowed. "Maggie," he said, pausing for a moment, "I'd like to ask you to have my child."

Maggie jumped as if touched by a red-hot poker. It was the most bizarre proposal she'd ever heard, and she'd heard some lulus in her time.

"Well?" Buddy asked hopefully. "What do you say?"

A billion thoughts and possibilities raced through her mind. She answered his question with a question of her own. "How much?"

"How *much*?!"

"Moneywise. How much will you pay me?"

What was she, some kind of mercenary? Start low, Buddy told himself. "Twenty-five thousand."

Maggie was no fool. She knew what he was up to. "No way," she said coolly. "A *hundred* thousand."

Buddy choked. "A *hundred* thousand?! You've got to be kidding."

"I'm serious, Mr. Evans. We're talking about human life here."

"*Fifty* thousand," Buddy said with finality in his voice. "Not one cent more."

Maggie bit her lower lip and nodded. "All right," she agreed. "Fifty-thousand dollars. For fifty thousand dollars I'll have your son."

Maggie extended her hand, and Buddy shook it. Each wondered in that same instant if they weren't perhaps making the mistake of their lives.

"Okay, we have a deal," Buddy said.

Maggie nodded. Her eyes wandered away from him and focused dreamily on the passing Manhattan skyline. She was not seeing Manhattan, though. She was seeing Paris.

Buddy studied her carefully. She was attractive—*very* attractive. Intelligent-looking, too. Not only that but she could drive a hard bargain and claimed to have musical talent as well. All well and good. But there were other questions to be asked, and Buddy had to ask them.

Before he could, though, Maggie suddenly turned and looked at him. "Do I have to live with you during the pregnancy?" she asked.

"In your own special area of the apartment," he answered. "I'm having the whole place redone. Don't worry, you'll like it."

"And you'll pay for everything?"

"The works," Buddy replied, glad to be talking business. "Food, clothing, expenses—it'll all be in the contract I have my lawyer draw up."

"How about French lessons?" she ventured. "I'm going to Paris next year."

"*French lessons?*" Buddy was too anxious to protest really. He grinned. "Oh, what the hell. You can have French lessons or whatever other lessons you want."

Buddy could feel the happiness of relief rushing through his body. He'd found a surrogate mother. He hoped.

The tour guide had moved down the deck and was continuing his spiel from only a few feet away. "Coming up pretty soon is gonna be Gracie Mansion, but before that you'll get a really good look at New York Hospital. I had my prostate done there. They do prostates better than anybody else in town. I call them the *crème de la crème* of prostates."

Buddy took a piece of paper out of his pocket. "I have a few things I need to ask you," he told Maggie, having to raise his voice to be heard above the tour guide.

"All right," Maggie said. "Ask away."

Buddy read from the list. "Have you ever had scarlet fever?"

"No."

"Mumps?"

"No."

"Measles?"

"No."

"High blood pressure?"

"High blood pressure?" A deep voice echoed.

Buddy and Maggie looked up. The tour guide was standing over them. "Go to Mount Sinai for high blood pressure. Or Flower Fifth. Good cardiac units. Whatever you do, though," he leaned in close and lowered his voice, "don't go to Jersey."

SEVEN

"I NEVER KNEW ANYBODY WHO GOT PREGNANT ON PURPOSE," said Cathy.

"You think I'm nuts, don't you?"

Maggie and Cathy were standing in the open doorway of a rehearsal room where Maggie's pupil, an exceptionally untalented ten-year-old, was forcing terrible sounds from his cello.

Cathy shook her head. "I think fifty thousand dollars is a lot of money," she said.

"I've gotta tell Renais whether I'm coming to Paris or not," Maggie explained. "The deadline's next week." She ran her fingers through her auburn hair and sighed, "I hate money."

At that moment, the boy made a noise with the cello like fingernails being scraped along a blackboard. Maggie winced and called across the room to him, "Go home, Leonard."

"I still got five minutes left," Leonard informed her and went on "playing." The little snot.

Maggie smiled at him through clenched teeth.

"Remember my friend Denise?" Cathy asked.

Maggie nodded.

"Well, when she needed money, she went on a TV game show."

"Yeah? What'd she win?"

"A year's supply of rug shampoo," Cathy frowned. "Then she had to go out and buy a rug."

Maggie smiled. "This guy seems pretty straight," she explained. "I mean, he's got his lawyer working up a contract and everything. It's strictly business, Cathy. There's nothing sexual."

On the word "sexual," Leonard stopped his sawing and cocked his head to listen. Aware that her ears were no longer being assaulted, Maggie turned and fixed a stern look on the boy.

"*Play,* Leonard," she instructed.

Reluctantly, Leonard resumed his "playing."

"I'm not saying you ought to try to get out of it," Cathy told Maggie. "Just be careful, that's all. Don't fall for this guy or anything like that."

"Relax," Maggie assured her friend. "I'm not stupid, you know. Anyway, this guy is the last guy in the world I'd fall for. He's supposed to be some kind of big playboy, but to tell the truth, *I* don't see what's so sexy about him."

On "sexy" Leonard stopped playing again.

"Leonard," Maggie whirled around. "Why don't you just go home?"

"I got two more minutes!" Leonard informed her.

"Then play."

Leonard put his bow to the cello and brought forth a sound not unlike that of a cat being strangled.

Maggie turned back to Cathy. "One good thing. No more Leonard."

"Just be careful," Cathy warned.

Celia staggered into the living room and dumped a heavy armload of library books onto the coffee table.

"That's all of 'em," she said with relief and dropped her tired bulk into an armchair. "Now you've got every damn book in the public library on havin' a baby."

Buddy, sprawled out on the couch and deeply engrossed in a huge volume, didn't look up. He just nodded and mumbled, "Thanks, Celia, you're a doll."

Celia sighed and kicked off her shoes. She looked around the room and frowned. There were library books all over the place. Literally dozens of them strewn about the room.

Buddy tapped the book in his hand. "This is fascinating stuff," he said, underlining a specific passage with a yellow Magic Marker. "Just listen to this—"

"I *already* know how babies are made," Celia said dryly. She indicated the dozens of books strewn about the room. "Why're you doin' all this readin' and studyin' on the subject? Why don't you just hop in the sack and *make* yourself one?"

She was trying to exasperate him again.

"We happen to be creating a child here," Buddy explained patiently. "We can't just 'hop in the sack' as you so elegantly put it. This is a scientific venture."

"Scientific venture?" she snorted. "Boy, you sure are a cold fish."

"Will you stop calling me that, please?" He pointed to the book in his hand. "Get this, now. It says that if you want to assure a male offspring, you should make love standing up."

"Standin' up?" Celia gaped at him. "Now I *know* you've lost all your marbles."

Buddy ignored her and read aloud from the book. " 'The reason being that the sperm carrying the male sex factor is stronger at first than the sperm carrying the female factor.' "

Celia shook her head. "The only factors I know about is when you hold a baby up and there's a 'factor' hangin' off it, it's a boy and if there ain't, it's a girl."

Buddy did a slow burn. "This is science," he insisted. "The male sperm swims uphill better than the female sperm."

"They havin' a race?"

"The female sperm, however, is more resilient in the long run, which is a credit to your sex, Celia."

Frowning, Celia stood and started out of the room, all the while eyeing Buddy like he was some kind of prize mental case. He heard her mumble something unintelligible as she passed through the doorway.

"What did you say?" he called after her.

No reply.

"I'll bet it was 'cold fish,'" Buddy said under his breath.

"Right on the nose!" came Celia's voice from the hall.

Buddy threw his book across the room.

EIGHT

MAGGIE HAD STARTED AN EXTRA SHIFT AT THE COFFEE shop, and she'd taken on what seemed like dozens of additional cello students. She was going to make the money come hell or high water. This Mr. Evans character still seemed pretty unreal. She couldn't count on him to come through with the "surrogate mother" job, although fifty thousand bucks for nine months work— or to put it more succinctly, nine months labor—was a dream.

Still, for the past few weeks she'd been working herself ragged. Besides the coffee shop and the lessons, there was Smog.

Smog's first record didn't exactly burn up the charts. But it did get some airplay, and as a result, the band got some extra gigs at clubs around town. Also one of the other songs from the album, "The Gall Bladder Blues," was becoming something of an underground hit.

This Friday Smog was going to be playing in the East Village. Maggie mustered what little strength she had left, dragged her electric guitar onto a southbound IRT, and decided how she was going to break the news to the group that it was all over.

She'd rehearsed this particular speech a hundred

times before. Because she was going to drop out of the band a hundred times before. But this time there was no question. She had to drop out. "Gall Bladder Blues" or not.

Johnnie's newest idea was gas masks for the group. They would appear on stage in these things and then rip them off when the announcer finished his introduction.

This time Maggie had a little trouble getting hers off. Billy had tied it too tight at the back, and she almost hyperventilated before she could start playing the first number.

Maggie watched the people in the club, dancing and clapping and shouting with the music. She felt so removed from all this. It was as if she were watching herself from a distance.

"Where are you going?" Johnnie asked, playing with the tubing on his gas mask.

"I'm taking off for a while."

Billy looked at her. "You gonna drop out of school?"

"Maybe. I don't know."

Maggie didn't explain about Mr. Evans. She was embarrassed. And besides, she didn't even know if anyone would believe her. So she did what any normal person would do in this situation. She lied.

"Look, I'm going to take care of this guy's kid, that's all."

"So why should that stop you from playing with the band?"

"He wants it to be a full-time job."

Billy smirked. "I thought you hated kids."

"I don't hate kids."

Billy figured he knew what the real story was.

"It's not the kid, is it?"

Maggie looked puzzled. "What do you mean?"

"I know," said Billy, nodding his head, "I know. It's the guy."

"What about him?"

66

Billy just kept staring at her as if he was trying to pin her down. "I know what's going on. You don't have to hide it."

"Hide what?"

Phones stepped into the argument here. She took both of Maggie's hands in hers.

"Hey, little lady, I'm a woman. I know about these things."

Billy was pissed. "You know jack shit."

Phones, undaunted, sat next to Maggie, still holding her hands. "The lady wants to quit the band. That's cool. That's jake. Everybody's got their own life to lead."

"Thanks, Phones," said Maggie.

Phones continued. "Many years ago there was this guru dude who lived way up on a mountaintop. Gurus hang out on mountain tops a lot. Anyway, this guru wakes up one day and looks out the door to his cave and sees that this other dude has walked all the way up the mountain to get wisdom from him. 'Hey, man, I come for wisdom.' 'You come to the right place,' says the guru. And he takes the man's hands and looks at them real close like."

Phones looked at Maggie's hands as the other two in the room stared silently and listened. For one thing, neither of them had ever heard Phones talk for so long.

"So this guru takes seven small stones and drops each one, one at a time, into the man's hand. He did this for seven years. Every day the guy would climb the mountain and the guru would drop seven small stones in his hand."

Phones paused.

"So what's it mean?" Maggie asked.

Phones shrugged. "I don't know. But it sounded good when I heard it."

Maggie shook her head as Johnnie embraced Phones. "Man, I didn't know you knew that many words."

Billy stared at Maggie angrily.

"I'm sorry, Billy. It's just something I have to do."

"Right," Billy muttered as he picked up his flute and oboe. "You go ahead and do it."

NINE

"MAGGIE MAY BE SORT OF NAIVE ABOUT THIS CONTRACT business," Buddy told Kurt as they stepped off the elevator, "so be careful to explain everything very slowly."

Before they could reach the doors to their offices, Whiplash Wilson, who had been lying in wait, was upon them, jabbering as usual. "Mr. Evans," he started, "are you aware that a Mr. John Bonkowski chipped a tooth on one of your drinking fou—"

"Oh, Whiplash," Kurt interrupted, "I think I just saw somebody trip on the escalator."

Without a split-second's hesitation, Whiplash instinctively took off down the hall at full speed.

Buddy paused before pushing open the door. "Maggie's young," he told Kurt, "so don't try to overpower her with any of your legalese."

"You talk about her like she's some kind of *child*."

"She's not a child. She's just naive."

Upon entering Buddy's office, they discovered Maggie seated on the couch beside a stern-faced, older woman. The older woman was wearing a tweed suit. And a scowl.

"Hi, Maggie," Buddy greeted her warmly. He was anxious to get this business over with. "You didn't tell me you were going to bring a friend along."

A faint smile formed on Maggie's lips. "This is Ms. Cannon," she explained. "My lawyer."

"Your lawyer?"

Ms. Cannon stood, reached out, and gripped Buddy's hand. She pumped it vigorously in a no-nonsense manner. "You're late, Mr. Evans," she said gruffly.

Buddy smiled. Ms. Cannon's face remained granite-like.

"Well," Kurt tossed his briefcase onto Buddy's desk, faced the assemblage, and smiled. Try to keep everything on a nice, friendly level, he reminded himself. He could already sense trouble. "Shall we go over the contract?" he asked cheerily.

"Not just yet," Ms. Cannon replied. She walked around behind the desk and dropped herself into Buddy's swivel chair. "Let's all sit down," she suggested.

Buddy sat down on the couch beside Maggie, feeling like a visitor in his own office. He had a good mind to throw that woman out of his chair. Who did she think she was?

Ms. Cannon pushed Kurt's briefcase to one side and opened her own. She removed a sheaf of papers which she spread out in front of her. "First of all," she said, "we'd like to get a psychological profile of Mr. Evans."

Kurt winced. He could feel a wave of heat coming from Buddy on the couch.

"What do you mean, a psychological profile?" Buddy wanted to know, trying his best to keep a check on his temper.

Maggie covered the smile that was growing on her face. It was obvious that Buddy Evans was used to being in the driver's seat. To see him otherwise was really quite humorous.

"I'd like to ask certain questions for the purpose of protecting my client," Ms. Cannon stated. "A psychological profile will be helpful."

Buddy sat back on the couch and frowned. He knew

it was useless to protest. "All right," he agreed wearily. "Go ahead. I have nothing to hide."

Ms. Cannon picked up the first sheet of paper in front of her and asked, "Homosexuality?"

"*What?*" Buddy sat upright.

"Sadomasochism?"

"*Sadomasochism?!*"

"Necrophilia?"

Buddy shot a look at Kurt. "That's disgusting," he said. "This whole *thing* is disgusting."

Ms. Cannon went right on. "Is there any history of insanity in your family?"

"Of course not!" Buddy snapped and turned to Maggie. "What are you asking me these questions for?"

"Well, you asked *me*," she replied sweetly. She could see the sweat beading on his forehead.

"But I didn't *know* you," Buddy whined.

"Well, I don't know you either."

"But I'm a respectable member of the community," Buddy protested. "I have an office. I have a secretary . . ."

"I'm sure a lot of necrophiliacs have secretaries," Maggie observed, managing to keep a straight face.

"Kurt," Buddy said, turning to his friend, "do I have to take this?"

Kurt was wishing he'd never gotten up that morning. "I think it's important to get things like this out in the open, Buddy," he said, trying to keep the peace. "Just calm down, pal."

"All right," Buddy said as he sat back and folded his arms against whatever these two ladies were going to throw at him next. "I'm calmed down. I'm very calmed down."

Ms. Cannon resumed. "My client and I would like to set a number of impregnation attempts before we start to charge additionally."

Buddy shook his head as if something had come

loose inside. He shot a quick look at Kurt who just shrugged.

"Charge additionally for *what*?" Buddy demanded.

"In case you fail," said Maggie. She couldn't wait to see his reaction to this.

"Fail?" repeated Buddy. "Me? Fail?" He turned to Kurt and both men exchanged knowing laughter. Buddy Evans fail? Were these two dames kidding? Buddy stared straight at Maggie. "I won't fail."

Ms. Cannon shrugged. "There are certain possibilities."

"Such as?" Buddy asked with a patronizing grin.

Ms. Cannon consulted her list. "Impotence. Sterility. Fetishism. Uh—"

Kurt jumped in. "Premature ejaculation." He nodded, proud to have added to the list. Then he felt Buddy's icy stare directed at him. He turned to Buddy and smiled weakly. "I was just speaking hypothetically, of course . . . er, uh, helping my fellow counselor. I, uh, why don't we continue, Ms., uh, Cannon?"

"That's not going to happen to me so why don't we just get that out of our minds?"

Ms. Cannon aimed a pencil at Buddy. "It has been known over the course of human history to happen."

"Not over the course of *my* history, ladies. Not over the course of my history."

"Well then, Mr. Evans," smiled Ms. Cannon, "you have something to look forward to."

"Not for another forty years, my dear counselor." Buddy turned to Kurt and whispered, "Do you believe this crap?"

"It's legal crap," explained Kurt, trying to get his friend and client to calm down.

"The next thing you know," said Buddy in his lowered voice, "they're going to ask me to drop my pants."

Ms. Cannon overheard him. She smiled. "I don't think that will be necessary."

Buddy glared at her. He wasn't sure if this was a compliment or an insult. But from a lawyer it could be both at the same time.

Buddy smiled and sat back. "Right now I have a few questions of my own to ask."

"You already asked me those," said Maggie, suddenly fearing the worst.

"I know I did. Health questions. But there are other areas, too."

"Such as?" Ms. Cannon demanded.

Buddy looked at her. "Do you believe in God?"

"Who?"

"God. You remember him."

Maggie faltered. "I, uh, sure. I guess I do. I think."

Buddy looked at Kurt. He smiled. "What do your parents do?"

"My father's dead."

Buddy jumped up. "Ah-ha!"

Maggie was puzzled. "Ah-ha! What?"

Buddy just nodded knowingly. "And your mother?"

"She's a psychologist."

"Ah-ha!"

"What's with the ah-has?"

"How often do you talk to your mother?" asked Buddy.

"Not very often. I mean she's a very busy lady. So am I." Buddy kept nodding as if he knew something.

"Who are your favorite painters?" asked Buddy.

Ms. Cannon interrupted. "I'm sorry, but I don't see the point of these questions—"

Maggie just stared at Buddy. "Modigliani. Klee. And Picasso." Buddy stared back at her.

"Are you now or have you ever been a member of the Communist Party?" Buddy winked at Kurt. Kurt had no idea what Buddy was getting at.

"No," said Maggie.

Buddy whispered to Kurt. "Just a ploy to get them off their guard. Get them a little confused."

Kurt, who couldn't figure out what Buddy was up to, nodded at Buddy. "It's working."

"Are you quite finished?" asked Maggie's lawyer.

"Maybe," answered Buddy. "Maybe. My lawyer will explain." He looked at Kurt.

Kurt cleared his throat. "Maybe." He had no idea what to say next. Then he looked down at the thick contract he was holding in his hand. "Oh, yes. The contract. Shall I point out some of the finer details in it?"

"Yes," said Ms. Cannon, "like the words."

"Good idea."

Kurt began to read the contract he had drawn up for Buddy. There wasn't much in his legal texts that he could draw upon. Not very much precedent in a case like this. But he did his best to make sure that all the angles were covered. And even though he was Buddy's lawyer, he wanted to make sure that Maggie was as protected as Buddy. Kurt believed that the law could deal with any problem. That's what he was told at Fordham. He had to remember that.

Four hours later, Buddy thought he could see light at the end of the tunnel.

"Furthermore," Kurt was reading aloud from the heavily amended contract, his voice reduced to a near croak, "the party agrees to live within the jurisdiction of said residence until the birth of the child and any unsupervised departure will result in breach of this contract . . ."

Kurt paused to swallow. His throat was killing him. Out of the corner of his eye, he caught a glimpse of Buddy sitting nearby on the couch, a dazed, zombielike expression on his face. The poor guy had really been through the wringer over the past few hours. He looked shell-shocked.

Maggie appeared to be a bit on the tired side herself. In fact, she was having a hard time keeping her eyes open. But as for Ms. Cannon, she was as alert as ever, listening carefully to each word of the contract.

"Lastly," Kurt pressed on, "the party agrees to surrender all rights after the birth of said child and under no circumstances shall she seek any such rights or privileges to the child for the child's natural life."

Kurt lowered the page and rubbed his neck. "That's it," he said, praying there'd be no further argument.

Maggie turned to her lawyer. Ms. Cannon nodded her head and said, "Sign."

Maggie reached across the desk and took the contract. Kurt handed her a pen. She hesitated for a moment—people have a tendency to do this sometimes when the thought that they might be ruining their lives occurs to them. But two other things occurred to Maggie—fifty thousand dollars and Paris. She signed her name on the indicated line.

"Buddy," Kurt said, "it's your turn."

Buddy blinked several times as if coming out of a deep sleep. "You mean," he asked hopefully, "it's all over?"

"We've agreed on every point," Kurt replied with satisfaction and pride. He couldn't wait to go out and have about a dozen martinis.

Buddy grinned happily and took the pen from Maggie. He made his scrawl in the appropriate space. Then he stood up and stretched his legs, tempted to let out a loud Tarzan yell of triumph. But instead he looked at Maggie and smiled. "Now all we have to do," he said, "is get you pregnant."

A strange uneasiness welled up inside Maggie. She'd done it. She'd signed. There was no turning back now. She returned Buddy's smile as best she could. "When do we get started?" Maggie asked meekly.

"Tonight," he replied.

TEN

THAT NIGHT IN HIS APARTMENT, BUDDY WAS DETER-
mined to make sure everything went perfectly. As he
saw it, every element of the evening had to be conducive
to achieving his goal—making a baby. The first thing
he'd done was give Celia the evening off. The last
thing he needed was her lurking about, waiting to am-
bush him.

Buddy carefully removed a long-playing record from
its jacket and placed it on the revolving turntable. Then
he straightened up and regarded his image in the living
room mirror. No doubt about it, he told himself, you
look great. Virile, in fact.

Buddy crossed the living room to the hallway. "You
about ready down there?" he called.

"I'm taking my temperature," Maggie's voice replied.

"How is it?"

"Just about right."

"Good." Buddy walked back to the stereo, tightening
the sash on his robe. "I'll just get the music ready." He
flicked the "on" switch, took a deep breath, and strode
purposefully into the hallway.

As he entered the bedroom, he noticed that the door
to the bathroom was slightly ajar. Maggie could be dis-
cerned inside at the sink, staring into the eyes of her
own reflection. Music suddenly swelled, and with it

came the sounds of the ocean. The squawk of sea gulls and the swish of the sea rumbled down the hallway and filled Buddy's bedroom.

"The soundman at the Garden got this record for me," Buddy explained even though he could not see her reaction. "Dr. Allen, in his book, says that natural sounds at the time of conception make all the difference in the world."

"What's the name of this record?" Maggie asked from inside the bathroom.

"It's called 'Sounds of the Great Sperm Whale in Love.'"

"My favorite," Maggie said dryly. Then she added nervously, "I'm almost ready."

Buddy was beginning to feel a bit nervous himself. But the nervousness, he assured himself, was just due to the excitement he felt. Not the excitement of sex— the excitement of the end result. Tonight might be the most important night of Buddy's life. Tonight might be the night that his son was conceived.

"Remember now," Buddy said, crossing over to the wall switch and lowering the lights, "there's nothing emotional about this evening and what we're about to do. This is merely a business transaction, right?"

"Check."

What was she *doing* in there?

Buddy went to the night table beside the bed, where a decanter and two wineglasses sat. He inspected the glasses, wiped a spot off one with the sleeve of his robe, then picked up the decanter and poured. Behind him, he heard the bathroom door open and then a soft, swishing sound—the sound of her nightgown.

"Here's me," Maggie announced hesitantly.

Buddy turned, and the fact that this evening was a "scientific venture" momentarily left his thoughts. Maggie looked quite stunning in the light nightgown. The somewhat nervous expression on her face only seemed to add to her appeal. Buddy quickly reminded himself that this was business.

"Would you like something to drink?" he asked, aware of the sudden dryness in his own throat.

"That would be nice," Maggie replied, clasping her hands together tightly in front of her. This was the most uncomfortable situation she'd ever been in. After all, how many times in your life are you hired to have a kid for somebody? How many times do you get yourself impregnated by a stranger?

Buddy extended one of the wineglasses to her. "How about we drink a toast?" He suggested. "A toast to success."

Maggie accepted the glass. "Okay. Success."

Buddy clinked his glass against hers and drank. Maggie lifted her own glass, took a swallow—and gasped. "What in the world *is* this?" she gagged.

"Gatorade," Buddy replied.

"Holy Christ!"

"It's for energy."

Maggie spit the remainder back into the glass. "Maybe you should let it breathe more," she said.

Buddy placed both glasses on the night table. He and Maggie were standing only a few feet apart. Under normal circumstances, Buddy wouldn't have had any trouble making his move. In this particular instance, however, he felt as awkward as a teenager trying to get up the courage to ask a girl to dance. Except, Buddy reminded himself, we're not going to be dancing.

"Well," he said self-consciously.

"Well," Maggie replied, hoping that the terror she felt was not showing in her eyes.

"I guess we should get this show on the road."

"I guess so."

Buddy reached out and took her by the hand. Then to Maggie's surprise, he led her past the bed and over to the wall on the other side of the room.

"What about the bed?" Maggie asked.

"Standing up," Buddy replied. "To insure a male child."

"Oh."

Buddy reached over and clicked off the light switch, plunging the room into darkness. The sounds of the sea continued to waft in from the hallway. Maggie expected to be hit by a wave any second now.

Gently, Buddy positioned her so that her back was against the wall. Then he deftly slipped her nightgown down over her shoulders. He moved closer, placed his hands on her hips, and moved against her.

"God," Maggie gasped, "it's really hard."

"Huh?"

"The wall. It's really hard."

"They're made that way."

"It's freezing, too."

He felt her shiver. "That's the mirror you're standing against. Here. Let me stand there."

Clumsily, they changed positions.

"God, it *is* cold," Buddy remarked.

For nearly a full minute, neither moved.

"Are you . . . ready?" Buddy finally asked.

"Check."

Buddy found his confusion growing. He wasn't sure how to proceed. It wasn't as though they were in love or just there for sex. Forge on, he told himself. Gently, he began to explore her body with his hands. Maggie found her attention being drawn elsewhere. To the other side of the room to be specific, where Buddy's aquarium was glowing phantomlike in the darkness. Floating on top of the tank was a dead fish. Buddy pressed against her.

"Oh, God," Maggie murmured. "It's just *lying* there."

"Well, give me a minute," Buddy said irritably. "I'm doing the best I can."

"I think it's dead."

"It might not be dancing, but it's not dead!"

"No, no," Maggie pointed past his shoulder. "Not you. Your fish."

"My *fish*?"

"In the aquarium. It's dead."

Buddy twisted his head around and regarded the floating fish. "Okay, it's dead," he said. "We'll hold services for it when we're through." He realized that whatever mood they'd had was now gone.

"Why don't we trade positions again?" Buddy asked. "That way you won't be tempted to look at the stupid fish."

Maggie agreed, and they switched stances again. Then Buddy began to move his hands about her body once more. The sounds of the sea were growing louder. Buddy moved against her, pressing their bodies together. Maggie was beginning to respond. Just as they seemed to be getting into it, Buddy mumbled, "It's so *limp*."

"I know," Maggie sighed, then suddenly realized that Buddy was now staring at the fish. He meant the *fish* was limp.

"Oh, for God's sake," Buddy disengaged himself, stalked over to the aquarium, and clicked off the florescent light.

"Can we just get this over with?" he asked in exasperation as he marched back to Maggie.

"Check."

But just as they moved together once more, a voice came over the stereo. "The Great Sperm Whale," it intoned dramatically, "is ready to make his desperate call across the blue void. . ."

"What's that?" Maggie whispered. "Who said that?"

"Ignore it. Just ignore it."

"Check."

"And stop saying 'check.' "

"It's clinical. I thought this was supposed to be clinical."

A loud bellow shook the room. "What the hell is

that?" Maggie cried out above the rumble, expecting the ceiling to cave in on them.

"It's a Great Sperm Whale," Buddy answered. "What did you think it was?"

"Well, excuse me," Maggie said, getting a grip on herself. "I guess I wasn't expecting to hear the world's largest mammal eighteen stories above Fifth Avenue."

Buddy let out a groan and stepped away from her. The mood had been destroyed again. It was hopeless.

"What's wrong?" Maggie asked.

"Put some clothes on," Buddy said.

"Why?"

"Just put some clothes on." Buddy shrugged on his dressing gown and crossed the room to the light switch. He flicked it on, illuminating Maggie as she slipped back into her nightgown. Buddy's face was a study in frustration and defeat.

"Will you tell me something?" Buddy asked.

"What?" There was a trace of annoyance in her voice, too.

"Are you doing this on purpose? Just to prolong your pleasure?"

Maggie stifled an urge to laugh in his face. She fixed him with an icy look instead. "No, Buddy," she answered. "I am not doing this just to prolong my pleasure."

Buddy sat down on the edge of the bed, looking beaten. Maybe the whole plan was wrong. Maybe he'd been wrong from the beginning.

"What's the matter?" Maggie asked, approaching him.

"Nothing's the matter."

"Just relax."

"I *am* relaxed," he said through clenched teeth.

"Try to get your mind off it. Think of something totally ridiculous."

"I can't."

"*I* can," Maggie said under her breath.

Buddy shook his head. "Maybe it's not clinical enough."

"That's the whole problem," Maggie informed him. "It's *too* damn clinical." Maggie sat down on the bed beside him. "Don't you have any . . . fantasies?"

"I don't need fantasies."

"Come on," she said, her voice growing conspiratory. "What about . . . *chains*?"

"God, no," Buddy said with a small chuckle. "I had a girlfriend once who tried that. For some reason, though, it didn't get me too excited. Everytime I looked at her, all I could think of was Kirk Douglas in *Spartacus*."

Maggie got up and retired to the bathroom, leaving the door open a crack in order to continue conversation. "You must have *some* fantasies," she said from within.

"Well . . . some," Buddy admitted warily.

"Like for instance?"

"I can't tell them to everybody," he explained defensively. "That's what makes them fantasies."

"Then I'll tell you one of mine. It's about—"

"I don't want to hear it."

"—a changing room in a department store."

Buddy perked up. "You have that one, too?" he asked incredulously.

"Yeah. With the curtain .on the booth that's too short—"

"No, no," Buddy jumped off the bed and approached the bathroom door. "Louver doors and you can see *feet* under them!"

"Tell me another one."

"Well," he said timidly, "there's the one where I'm Zorro. You know, with the mask and the black cape and everything."

"That sounds exciting. Tell me about it."

"Well, there's not much to tell really. But at the end I make a big 'Z' on the wall."

"With your sword?"

"Of course with my sword. What did you think?"

"I thought maybe . . . never mind. Got any more?"

Buddy thought for a moment, then broke into a sheepish grin. "There's the one where I'm Superman."

"You do it in a phone booth, right?"

"Better than a phone booth. We do it in the sky over Metropolis."

"In the *sky?*"

"Yeah," he said. "Right in front of the *Daily Planet* building. Pretty good, huh?"

"Yeah, I like that one myself." She thought it over. "In the sky." Then she shook it out of her mind. "But what's your most *secret* fantasy. You know, the one that might actually come true some day?"

Buddy leaned back against the wall and stared dreamily up at the ceiling. "The one with the mysterious lady."

"Who is she?"

"I don't know," he shrugged. "That's why she's so mysterious. Anyway, I see her from a distance. In a bar. A smoky, sultry bar. And I—"

"Drool?"

"I watch her from a distance." Buddy was getting lost in his own imagination. "She keeps turning down other men. Then . . . she eyes me from across the room, blows a puff of smoke across her table, and mouths a kiss to me."

The bathroom door suddenly flew open, and Maggie emerged fully clothed and looking determined. She slung her bag over her shoulder and headed for the door to the hall. "Meet me at the Plaza Hotel in one hour," she ordered. "In the Oak Bar."

"Huh?"

"One hour."

Before Buddy could sputter back a response, Maggie was gone. He heard her footsteps disappearing down the hallway, followed by the sound of the front door opening and closing.

"The Oak Bar," Buddy said aloud. "That's smoky and sultry . . ."

Buddy turned and caught a look at himself in the wall mirror. He was genuinely surprised to see the lecherous smile that was spreading across his face.

ELEVEN

ALMOST AN HOUR LATER, MAGGIE WAS SITTING IN A corner at the Oak Bar. The smoke was thick enough to dim the lights on the walls.

Three salesmen, in New York from Texas for a stationery convention, sat around the table next to Maggie's. After much deliberation, the bravest—and drunkest—of the three gave the thumbs up salute to his friends and turned to face Maggie. He leered politely.

"Hi there, pretty lady," he drawled, "that's a lovely fragrance you're wearing. What's it called?"

Maggie stared icily into his eyes. "Estrogen."

The Texan paused for a moment, then leaned closer. "French, huh?"

Maggie wanted to turn this redneck off once and for all. "I don't speak any English," she said.

The Texan turned back to his friends and shrugged. They laughed as their Don Juan adjusted his tie.

Outside Buddy was just arriving in a taxi. He overtipped the driver and overtipped the doorman who helped him out. He even held out a dollar to an elderly female guest coming out of the Palm Court. He walked to the Oak Bar and entered. The room was crowded. He looked over the heads of the many conventioneers and theater-goers. The whole place was a blur. But then he noticed something, and what he saw made his heart skip a beat. Sitting all alone at a table across the room was a woman. Not just any woman. *The* woman. The woman who comes to mind when you think of words like "stunning" or "captivating." And also, for the most part, "unattainable." She had dark brown hair tied up behind her head. But several wisps of hair hung down in all the right places like the wrapping on a package. If you pulled one of the wisps, all the hair would come tumbling down. Her eyes were also dark with just a touch of the exotic about them. You could easily imagine that someone in her family had come from an island a long time ago. Her mouth was a perpetual pout. But not a spoiled pout. A little girl's pout that was instantly ready to smile. Buddy caught himself staring at her. Then an amazing thing happened. The woman—*The* woman—was looking at Buddy. Her pout turned into a shy smile. Buddy froze.

"Oh, come on," he told himself, "it's a woman. You know about them. They don't make you go all to pieces like this anymore." He was lying and he knew it.

He found himself walking to her table. Then he found himself standing in front of her table. She smiled.

"I've been waiting for you, big boy."

"You have?"

She stared directly into his eyes. Awkwardly he shifted his gaze. And into that gaze came another incredible sight. Maggie. Maggie was sitting in an opposite corner. And she looked exquisite. She blew him a silent kiss.

"Are you just going to stand there or are you going to sit down and make me happy?" the other woman asked, breaking Buddy's focus on Maggie.

"Huh?"

The mystery lady smiled. "Anyone ever tell you that you got a great way with words?"

"Me?"

She nodded yes. "You."

Buddy stammered. "I went to college. I know all about words."

This was too much. Here he was. In the Oak Bar. Pursuing a lifelong fantasy. And after a lifetime of dreaming and hoping, he had her. Only there was one problem. There were two of them. It must be a kind of punishment, he figured. My parents must have done something very wrong.

Buddy's attention went back to Maggie. She lifted a finger and motioned that he should come to her table. Buddy looked at the mysterious woman in front of him.

"You won't believe this," he started to explain.

"Try me."

He wanted to. He wanted to very much. Of course, he realized she was a hooker. And she probably charged a fortune. He wanted to ask her if she took credit cards, but something kept drawing his attention back to Maggie. She really did look wonderful. He'd never looked at her in this light before. Or this lack of light. Maybe it was the way she stared at him. Or the way she arched one eyebrow. Or maybe it was the faint smile. . . .

"Would you like me to sit down?" Buddy offered, having torn himself away from the mysterious brunette and aware that he and Maggie were being watched by the three dumbstruck salesmen.

Maggie shook her head no.

"Would you like a drink?"

Again she shook her head no. Then her hand moved up and slightly parted the front of her overcoat. Buddy's mouth dropped open. She was completely naked underneath!

The three salesmen couldn't see anything from their angle, but the expression on Buddy's face was all they needed. They craned their heads forward to catch his next words.

Buddy tried to regain control of his facial muscles,

but he had a hard time tearing his eyes away from Maggie's nakedness. Finally he found his way back to reality. He noticed the three salesmen waiting eagerly for him to speak.

Buddy raised his voice for their benefit. "Would you like to go upstairs and make a baby?" he asked Maggie.

"I thought you'd never ask," she replied, and the three salesmen nearly fell off their chairs. "I'm in 312," she added.

Buddy nodded. Maggie closed the front of her overcoat, turned, and sashayed out of the bar. Buddy nonchalantly straightened his tie. Then he gave a wink to the three salesmen who all looked like they'd been turned to stone. Smiling with anticipation, Buddy left the bar.

"Jesus H. Christ," breathed the salesman who'd tried to hit on Maggie a few minutes before. "Did you hear that? So *that's* how they do it in New York. I gotta try this out."

Drunkenly, he got off his stool and lurched into the path of a young woman passing by. She stopped. He'd given her no choice.

"Would you like to sit down?" he asked her.

"No."

"Would you . . . like a drink?"

"No."

"Would you . . . like to go upstairs and make a baby?"

She took the highball glass out of his hand and poured its contents over his head.

Buddy couldn't have been more pleased with Room 312. It was definitely conducive to fantasy. High ceiling. Low lights. Romantic music playing softly. Buddy found himself standing in the middle of the room, reminding himself that this wasn't a dream—it was really happening. And that meant he wasn't going to wake up just when it was getting good.

Maggie, still playing her vamp role to the hilt, sauntered over to him after closing the door and slowly began to undo his tie. She made the act as sensuous as possible. Unfortunately, she made the mistake of yanking the wrong end, which caused the tie to tighten unexpectedly. Buddy let out a cough and quickly reached up to loosen it himself. Maggie stood in front of him and stared. Over her shoulder, he could see the lights of the city. The northern view looked out over the park and along Fifth Avenue. The flickering uptown lights shone in the distance beyond the park.

Buddy pulled the tie from his neck and threw it across the room. He didn't see where it landed. He didn't care. What the hell? It was just a tie. In front of him was a lifelong fantasy.

In the half-light of the room, Maggie's face appeared half a girl's and half a woman's. She was very beautiful. Maybe not in the same way that most of Buddy's women friends were, but certainly in a more interesting way. Maggie's beauty had angles to it, degrees of beauty. In one light she looked one way. In another light she looked very different. Like a diamond. There was certainly nothing artificial about this face. It changed. It probably even grew on you.

Buddy felt his trousers slipping to the floor. "I feel like I'm fourteen years old."

And he looked it, too.

TWELVE

MAGGIE AWOKE IN BED WITH A WARM FACE.

She blinked. Sunlight was streaming in on her through the window. For a few seconds she was totally disoriented. She knew that she was not home in her *own* bed, so where the hell was she?

She didn't have to wonder long. The sight of Buddy on the other side of the hotel room sound asleep on the sofa told her instantly where she was and what she was doing there. And more importantly, it reminded her of what had transpired last night.

Maggie felt an odd flash of disappointment. Disappointment because he was over there sleeping on the couch and not in the double bed beside her. But that feeling went away quickly. Why should she expect to wake up beside him? After all, what had happened last night in that bed was strictly a business transaction. Nothing more, nothing less.

Business transaction? The words brought the trace of a smile to Maggie's lips. She could recall a good thirty minutes or so last night that didn't have anything to *do* with business.

Buddy grumbled in his sleep and altered his position slightly. He looked about to fall off the couch. Maggie wondered whether she shouldn't get up and try to do something about it. Oh, what the hell, she figured. Let him fall. She knew that when he woke up he'd be the same business-as-always Buddy Evans. She knew the type. He'd wake up, smile politely, maybe take her to breakfast, but never once would he mention the passion that had grown between them in that bed. Maggie had a good mind to go over there and *help* him fall off that couch.

Instead she just lay back and stared at the ceiling. The deal had been consummated. Now it was up to nature to take *its* course.

Maggie waited to feel pregnant.

THIRTEEN

DR. LAWRENCE LIEBEGOTT'S WAITING ROOM WAS FULL. There wasn't a magazine left on the rack. A young man in overalls was reading *Mechanix Illustrated,* several young ladies shared the *Cosmopolitan*s and the *Vogue*s, and the few elderly men and women swapped jokes from *Reader's Digest*. Obviously, Dr. Liebegott's practise was diversified. He called himself a general practitioner even though he was informed by the two younger doctors who shared his suite of offices that that term was antiquated. Good, thought Larry, I'm antiquated, too.

There was one man in the waiting room who wasn't reading. Buddy Evans paced nervously in front of the nurse's desk, stopping every thirty seconds to ask her if Larry had called for him to come into the office. Larry was in there with Maggie, and although he wasn't her official doctor for the pregnancy, Buddy wanted Larry to oversee the whole "operation." Larry was glad to oblige, fully aware that Buddy's sensitivity was not always his strongest characteristic. Larry had the test results sent to his office. He wanted to be the one to tell Maggie if she were pregnant or not. Buddy, he figured, might leave the news on a note Scotch-taped to the toaster. Or on the telephone answering machine. That would be like Buddy.

"Doesn't Dr. Liebegott want to see me now?"

The nurse didn't smile this time. "No."

"Are you sure?"

"Yes."

Buddy paced. He stopped in front of a middle-aged woman who was reading *Better Homes and Gardens*. She looked up at him.

"It's my first child," Buddy explained to her. "I'm a little nervous."

The lady smiled. "Isn't that nice? When's it due?"

Buddy shrugged. "Nine months, I guess."

The lady's smile died. She quickly went back to her article on extramarital affairs among migrant farm workers.

Buddy paced on. "Any word yet?"

"No."

He stopped in front of the young man in overalls.

"Got a cigarette, pal? I'm a bit nervous. I'm expecting my first kid."

The young man held out his cigarette pack. "Camels okay?"

Buddy shook his head. "No thanks, I don't smoke."

He must be on something, thought the young man.

In the office, Maggie stared at Larry's diplomas. The big red drops of wax on each one reminded her of the countless blood tests she'd just gone through.

"Do you tell him or do I?" Larry asked. Maggie liked this man. She liked his soft voice and fatherly manner. In fact, he looked a little like her father. The same weathered but pleasant face. The same thinning gray hair.

"I suppose I should tell him," Maggie replied.

Larry tipped back in his swivel chair and rested his feet on the desk top. "You know, Maggie," he began, wondering to himself how many times he'd made the following statement, "pregnancy can change things in a woman. And I don't mean just physically."

"I know," Maggie nodded, wondering to herself how

many times Larry had made that statement to his patients. Thousands of times? Millions?

"I want you to know, Maggie, that you can come in
here and talk to me anytime."

"Thanks," she said gratefully. She had a feeling that in
the months ahead she'd be taking advantage of that
offer.

Larry leaned forward and gave her his best fatherly
smile. He was not unaware of the fact that his patients
looked at him in a paternal manner. "I like you," Larry
admitted. "I don't want you to think of me as the 'other
side' just because Buddy happens to be a good friend of
mine."

"Thanks," Maggie said. She meant it. She could use
an ally. In the past few weeks she'd begun to feel that
people were ganging up on her. "Have you known
Buddy a long time?" she asked.

"Pretty long."

"I was just wondering," Maggie began, searching for
the right words. "I think he's a very nice man and
all—funny and well-mannered—but . . . has he always
been so . . . emotionless?"

Larry took his legs down from the desk top and
looked at her. "Did you know he was married before?"

"No," she answered with surprise. Buddy didn't
seem like the type.

"He never talks about it," Larry explained, his voice
lowered as if Buddy might be able to hear. "He was
young and he got burned pretty bad."

"I didn't know anything about it."

"Well, he never talks about it. You see, Buddy keeps
a lot of stuff bottled up inside him. I think he's afraid of
letting it out . . . afraid he'll get stung again. So don't
think he's an iceberg. It's all there. He just keeps it
buried. He's a very wonderful guy. But don't tell him I
told you any of this because that wonderful guy might
just kill me."

"I won't tell," Maggie promised, digesting the information. "This sort of puts a different light on things. Maybe I should—"

She never got the chance to finish her sentence. Unable to contain himself in the waiting room, Buddy burst in through the door, jabbering excitedly like a disc jockey on speed. "It worked, right? Did it work? I know it did. It had to work. Didn't it? Didn't it work?"

Buddy was bobbing around the room like Muhammad Ali, looking from Larry's face to Maggie's, then back again. Larry just gave him a bored, vacant stare.

"You can't fool me," Buddy told him. "I've seen that look on your face before. I know what it means. It means it worked."

"You seem pretty sure," Maggie observed. She was beginning to find his cockiness rather irritating.

Buddy grinned triumphantly and pointed to Maggie. "Just look at those rosy cheeks. There's a kind of *glow* about her. It worked, didn't it, Larry?"

"The rabbit died," Larry answered.

"It did? Really?" Buddy's face lit up with excitement. He whirled around to Maggie. "What did I tell you? I was right! The rabbit died!" Buddy ran to the door and threw it open. "The rabbit died!" he shouted to the surprised people outside in the waiting room. "The rabbit died!"

Maggie decided she'd had enough of his idiocy. She got out of her chair and marched toward the door. She might have made it out right then if Buddy hadn't suddenly turned back and blocked her path.

"Maggie," he said with a stupidly ecstatic smile on his face, "the rabbit *died*!"

Maggie fixed him with a sarcastic look. "I asked them if I could have the ears," she said, "but all they'd give me was the *tail*." She thrust the wadded cotton ball she'd been holding into his hand and stormed out.

Mutely, Buddy stared down at the furry whiteness in his hand, then looked across the room at Larry who was regarding him with a pained expression. "What's the matter with *her*?" Buddy asked.

"Buddy," Larry said, trying to be patient, "you're a great guy. You're probably my best friend . . ."

"Gee, thanks," Buddy smiled, genuinely touched.

"But sometimes," Larry continued, "sometimes, Buddy, you're the biggest lunkhead who ever walked the face of the earth."

Buddy was startled. "I *am*?"

"You are."

"Oh." Buddy's face was knotted with confusion.

"You've heard of dying with dignity?" Larry asked.

"Yeah."

"Well, try living with some. That girl's a human being, you know, not some kind of baby machine."

Buddy let out a long sigh and nodded. He dropped himself into the chair Maggie had vacated. "I guess I have been acting like a jerk lately," he admitted. "I'll try to be more considerate. She'll be moving into the apartment next week. I'll make it a point to think of her as a human being."

"Good."

Buddy vowed to himself to be more considerate. But he quickly put the thought out of his mind as another one wormed its way back in.

"Pregnant," he said with a wide grin spread across his face. "Can you believe it?"

Larry nodded. "I can believe it."

Buddy then became serious. He walked up close to Larry and took him by both shoulders. "We did it, Larry. We did it." Buddy shook him like a comrade-at-arms and marched out of the office.

The first few months were bizarre to say the least. Buddy wasn't used to having a roommate, and here he was with one who he was paying to carry his child—an attractive young woman he had impregnated but did not love. Their relationship was strained at best. And terribly formal. Neither one knew quite how to relate to the other. Mostly, they would just act pleasant, crack nervous jokes, and try to stay out of each other's way. Fortunately, Celia was around most of the time to serve as buffer and middleman.

Maggie had the house to herself during the day while Buddy was at work. Her schedule consisted of getting up late, practicing her music for a couple of hours in the morning, and watching soap operas with Celia in the afternoon—except the soaps that dealt with unwanted pregnancy. For a while this life came as a welcome vacation, having nothing to do after the busy and hectic schedule she'd been used to. But after a while, Maggie began to grow edgy and restless.

She forgot about dating—it seemed uncomfortable in her present condition. She concentrated mostly on the baby growing inside her and gradually began to enjoy the changes it was putting her body through. Sometimes she found herself wondering what the child would be like after it was born—when she was gone. These thoughts would eventually begin to get her down, and to fight them she would lose herself in her music or go out for long walks with Cathy.

Buddy's life changed considerably. His days at work were pretty much routine, the only addition being sundry calls during the day to check on Maggie. Most evenings he spent home in the apartment. Overnight one of the city's busiest playboys changed into a complacent homebody. There were times, of course, when he'd call up a woman and go out for a night on the town, but his heart was rarely in it. He preferred spending his evenings at home, reading baby books and watching Maggie out of the corner of his eye. He tried his best not to overdo the watchful mother-hen act, but he often gave in and would overwhelm Maggie with endless questions about how she felt, what the baby felt like inside her, was she following her diet and her exercises, and so forth.

Though Buddy sometimes would take Maggie out to dinner or a movie, their relationship remained formal and businesslike. It was oddest when they returned home at night, each to retire after a pleasant "good night" to their respective bedrooms.

Under different circumstances, they might even have been attracted to one another in the way that opposites often attract. But these circumstances were anything but ordinary, and as far as each was concerned, love was out of the question. They began to feel like two prisoners who shared the same cell. Each wondered how long they could keep it up. Nine months was a long time—and it was not passing quickly.

FOURTEEN

MAGGIE COULD'NT COMPLAIN ABOUT THE LIVING QUAR-
ters he'd provided. Her room was bright, spacious, and
quite beautiful. Moreover, Buddy had been absolutely
forbidden to cross its threshold without a personal in-
vitation. In the two months she'd been there, Maggie
had not once allowed him to enter. Of course, Buddy
hadn't asked. He respected her privacy, and Maggie
appreciated it. There were only two objects in the
room that reminded Maggie why she was living in
Buddy Evans' apartment—an exercise bicycle and a
doctor's scale.

Inside her room, Maggie could do as she pleased.
But elsewhere she was beginning to feel that her life
was not her own, that she was a puppet in the hands of
Buddy Evans. Not that he ordered her around or yelled
at her or anything like that. Quite the opposite. Most of
the time he was friendly, gentle, and sweet. His effect
on her was subtle . . . but it was working. Not that there
was anything malevolent about him, but as the baby
grew inside her, Maggie began to feel oppressed, and
when she felt that way, she had to blame *somebody*.
Buddy was the perfect target.

As the days passed, one seemed to blur into the next
—it was difficult for Maggie to tell them apart. The
same little dramas were acted out night after night . . .

Buddy sat at the dinner table, his attention fixed on a paperback book entitled *Naming Your Child,* clenched tightly in his hand. He'd barely touched his steak and French fries.

This last fact, however, did not escape Maggie, who was sitting at the other end of the table, her own plate sparsely populated with bean sprouts. Bean sprouts. She'd really begun to hate those things. Not to mention the *other* things that had been decided upon for her diet. She fought back an impulse to stab his sirloin with her fork and down it with one quick gulp.

Celia, sitting nearby and working on her own steak, caught Maggie's eye and gave her a sympathetic frown. The two had become great friends over the past few weeks, coconspirators in the constant battle against Buddy Evans. "Sorry, honey," Celia said, feeling a little guilty.

"It's okay." Maggie nudged her bean sprouts with her fork. "I agreed to stick to the diet, and that's what I'm gonna do."

Buddy looked up from his reading and smiled. "Maggie, did you have something from the bread group today?"

"Yes."

"What?"

"Bread."

Satisfied, Buddy nodded and went back to his studying. Maggie went back to pushing bean sprouts. No one spoke for nearly a full minute. Then Buddy broke the silence.

"How about . . . Erasmus?" He peered over the top of the book at Celia and Maggie, studying their reactions.

"*Erasmus?*" Maggie repeated. "What kind of a name is *that*?"

"You know what it means?" Buddy asked.

"I'll tell you what it means," Celia chimed in. "It

means with a dumb name like that the kid ain't gonna have any friends."

Buddy frowned but was undaunted. "I've got another one I like," he said. "Salisbury!"

"Sounds like a steak," Celia muttered, taking a mouthful of her own.

"It's English," Buddy explained. "It means 'from the guarded place.' "

Celia ignored him and cut another piece of steak. "Men always got the craziest ideas about naming kids," she remarked to Maggie. "You take *my* husband. He wanted to name our first son Theophilus. Can you imagine that?"

"Why Theophilus?" Maggie asked.

Celia grinned. " 'Cause when he first got a look at him, he said, 'That's Theophilus-lookin' baby I've ever seen!' "

Maggie and Celia laughed.

Buddy shook his head. "I don't think the two of you are getting into the proper spirit of this," he observed, scanning another page. "Here we go," he said suddenly. "Shalot. It means 'wind that passes in the night.' "

" 'Wind that passes in the night,' " Maggie repeated. "Why don't you just call him *Fart*?"

Celia howled at that one. Buddy began to do a slow burn. "Very funny," he said under his breath. "I just hope the kid isn't born with your sense of humor."

Celia speared a piece of steak and started to lift it mouthward when she felt Maggie's hungering eyes upon her. Celia looked up. Sure enough, Maggie was staring at the piece of steak on the end of the fork, nearly drooling with desire. Her heart went out to the girl.

Celia shot a look over at Buddy. He was immersed in the book. Deftly, she thrust her fork across the table and dropped the piece of meat onto Maggie's plate. Maggie looked at it like a starving dog who'd just been tossed a bone. But before Maggie's fingers could pick it up, Buddy's hand suddenly snaked out in front of her and snatched it away.

Maggie nearly burst into tears. "It's such a *little* piece," she protested, sounding all of three years old. "Come on," she begged. "Please? Pretty please?"

Buddy stood his ground. He didn't like being task-master, but he figured it had to be done. "You've already had your hi-protein group for this meal."

"*What* hi-protein group?"

"The boiled egg you ate."

"You call that a *group*?" Maggie demanded. "One lousy boiled egg is a *group*?"

Buddy popped the piece of steak into his own mouth. "It's part of the deal, Maggie," he reminded her. "You have to follow the rules."

Buddy went back to his reading. Looking down, Maggie discovered that she had picked up her butter knife and was clenching it tightly in her hand. She wondered if it was possible to kill a man with a butter knife.

FIFTEEN

HANGING AROUND THE APARTMENT AND BORED BEYOND endurance one afternoon, Maggie had a sudden brilliant idea. The more she thought about it, the more sense it made. She switched off *Love of Life,* grabbed her coat, and caught a cab to Madison Square Garden (not, it should be pointed out, in the hope of seeing Buddy). She was actually hoping that she wouldn't run into him at all.

What better way to figure out the man than to have a look around the premises of the place that seemed to possess his heart and soul twenty-four hours a day? He was always so damned secretive about himself that even though Maggie had been in his company for several months now, she still hadn't a clue as to what the guy was really like. She wanted some idea as to the personality of the man whose child she was carrying. Oh, sure, he was pleasant enough on the surface, but Maggie wanted to find out what really made Buddy Evans tick. She figured the answer might lie within the walls of the Garden.

To Maggie, Madison Square Garden was as alien as the dark side of the moon. She'd never even been inside a sports arena, enclosed or otherwise. Her own experience was limited to concert halls and musical auditoriums.

The Garden was an entirely different matter. Maggie had found herself strangely fascinated by the place ever since she first discovered that Buddy ran it. Previously it seemed to her that the Garden's main function was providing a setting where men in their undershorts could beat each other up with boxing gloves or run up and down a court, stuffing balls through hoops—all to the delight of several thousand paying customers. It was Maggie's conclusion that it was all pretty ridiculous. But then, Maggie had never been capable of figuring out what all the fuss was about when it came to sports, competitive or otherwise. In her family, exercise consisted of Sunday afternoon classical jam sessions—mother at the piano, father on saxophone, younger sister on flute, and Maggie on cello.

Maggie paid the cab driver and took a couple of steps across the pavement. She stopped and gazed up at Madison Square Garden, feeling puny beneath its overpowering facade. There was something distressingly "male" about the place, something impenetrable. Madison Square Garden is one of the largest auditoriums in the world, she thought to herself, and the man who was responsible for running it had hired her to have his child. Go figure it.

Steeling herself for the task ahead, Maggie pushed through one of the main doors and was pleasantly relieved to find no guards in sight. Probably off catching a smoke, she figured. Maggie looked around for the proper direction to take. Her recollection of the Garden's layout was faint at best—she hadn't remembered much from her first and only visit when she'd come with Ms. Cannon to sign the contract.

She passed a couple of janitors sweeping the floor and headed toward the mezzanine level. Maggie first wanted to get an overview of the place before she went snooping about, seeking out the bits and pieces of Buddy that she suspected were hidden about.

Tad loved being alone on the court. He loved the

echo of his squeaking sneakers and the reverberation of the bouncing basketball. In just a few hours, he realized, the entire auditorium would be full to capacity with screaming fans, their attention riveted to the court he now stood upon. Tad dribbled over to the foul line, set himself, and shot—a perfect swish. He chased the ball down, returned to the foul line, and shot again— perfect swish number two.

Maggie slowly came down the mezzanine steps and stood against the rail, gazing down at the basketball court that had been set up for the evening's Knicks game. She was fascinated by the small boy who was making shot after shot. She marvelled at his concentration.

They were quite alone, the two of them, though the boy did not know he had company at first. But after a few moments, sensing her eyes upon him, Tad whirled around and suddenly looked up. Maggie, taken by surprise, managed to smile at him.

"Hello there," she said pleasantly, hoping she hadn't disturbed him.

"Hi," the boy replied, somewhat cautiously. He held the basketball out in front of him. "Wanna shoot with me?"

"I'm not very good at it," Maggie confessed.

"I'll show you," Tad said, smiling. He was a genuinely friendly kid. "Come on down. It's easy."

A few minutes later, Maggie was starting across the court to join him when Tad called to her, "Better take your shoes off. Uncle Buddy'll get real pissed off if he sees you on the court in street shoes."

Maggie stopped in her tracks and looked at him quizzically. "Uncle Buddy?"

"He runs this place," Tad replied. "He and my dad."

Maggie kicked her shoes off and slowly walked across the court. "Buddy Evans is your uncle?" she inquired.

"Well, he's not my *real* uncle," Tad confessed.

Maggie nodded. "Your dad's name wouldn't be Kurt, would it?"

"Kurt?" Tad looked perplexed for a second, then brightened. "Oh yeah," he said. "That's my dad's *other* name."

Maggie was beginning to get nervous. "Is Buddy around here someplace?" she asked, searching the stands.

"They're upstairs in a conference or something," Tad answered. He was regarding her with great interest. "Wait a minute," he said suddenly, breaking into a wide grin. "I know who you are. You're having Uncle Buddy's baby!"

Maggie felt a cold shiver run through her body. "Your dad told you about Buddy and me?" She was genuinely shocked.

"Well, he and my mom think I don't know," Tad confessed. "But I always listen to them when they think I've gone to bed. That's when you hear the best stuff."

Maggie nodded. This kid was no dope. "I'll bet you think the whole thing's kinda weird," she said.

Tad shrugged. "I dunno. I like to make funny noises with my armpit," he reasoned. "People think *that's* weird."

"*I* don't think that's so weird."

Tad grinned and lifted his arm. "Wanna hear one?" he asked excitedly.

"Uh, better not," Maggie said. "There's a pretty big echo in here."

"I guess you're right." Tad picked up the basketball that he'd trapped between his feet and took a couple of dribbles. "You wanna play horse?" he asked.

"Maybe in a minute," Maggie replied. There was something on her mind. "Can I ask you something . . . ?"

"Tad," he said and extended his hand.

Maggie shook it and smiled. "My name's Maggie."

"I know."

"What I want to ask you is . . . what do you *really* think about what Buddy and I are doing?"

"I'm just a kid," Tad admitted. "But I think Uncle Buddy would make a great dad."

"You like him, don't you?"

"Yeah, he's really nice." Tad paused for a moment. Something had just entered his mind. "The thing I don't get is how come he didn't *marry* you?"

"He doesn't want a wife. He just wants a son."

"Why?"

"Well, some people aren't right for marriage," Maggie suggested tactfully. "Like Uncle Buddy, I guess."

Tad studied her. Then his face began to turn crimson and he stared down at the floor. "I think Uncle Buddy's dumb," he said quietly. "I think you'd be great to be married to."

Maggie blushed, surprised but at the same time flattered by the boy's candor. "Tad," she said, "you're gonna be a real lady-killer some day."

To cover his embarrassment, Tad took the basketball and tossed it at the hoop. He missed by a mile. He and Maggie stood at the foul line and watched the ball bounce into the bleachers, neither one speaking or making a move to go after it.

"What's gonna happen?" Tad finally asked.

"What do you mean?"

"To you. After the baby gets born."

Maggie shrugged. "I guess I'll just fade away."

Tad shook his head. "Uncle Buddy's missing the boat," he said sadly.

Maggie laughed and gave the boy a hug. Although embarrassed, Tad managed to respond. He noticed a marked difference between Maggie's hug and, say, his grandmother's.

"Okay, you two, break it up."

Maggie and Tad parted at the sound of the voice.

It was Kurt. He was standing just a few yards away, smiling. "Hi, Maggie," he said as he approached. "I take it you two have met."

"I think Maggie's real neat," Tad confessed to his dad.

"Looking for Buddy?" Kurt asked her.

"No," Maggie replied. She wasn't sure whether or not Kurt was somebody she could trust yet. "I was in the neighborhood and I thought I'd drop in for a look."

Kurt shot a look at Tad. Tad grinned at him. "I know everything," the boy admitted.

Kurt raised an eyebrow. "And I'll bet you've been asking poor Maggie all kinds of questions, right?"

"I only have *one* question," Tad replied. "How come Uncle Buddy's so dumb?"

"You've got a great kid," Maggie told Kurt.

Kurt smiled. "I think so, too," he said and draped an arm around his son's shoulder. "And you know something?" he asked, bending his head down to Tad's ear. "I think he's dumb, too."

The three of them laughed, but before anyone could speak, they were interrupted by the echo of heels crossing the court.

"What's going on here?" Buddy asked as he joined them. He was smiling, but it was evident that he suspected some kind of conspiracy in the works. He'd also forgotten to take his shoes off, breaking Buddy's cardinal rule number one.

"I wanted to tell you something," Maggie lied. "Celia's gonna be off tomorrow night, and I thought I'd fix dinner myself."

"You came here to tell me that?" Buddy asked with a certain trace of relief in his voice. He was afraid she'd come to drop a bomb on him.

"I was in the neighborhood," Maggie replied.

Buddy nodded. "Fine," he said. "But nothing fattening. I think you're putting on too much weight."

"Oh, darn," Maggie pretended to be disappointed. "And I thought we'd order out from MacDonald's."

Buddy forced a chuckle. He knew she was giving the needle. "I hate to call an end to this little get-together," he said, looking at his watch, "but we've got work to do, Kurt."

"Can't you shoot some baskets with me?" Tad implored.

"Oh, yes," Maggie insisted. "*Do* shoot some baskets, Buddy. I'll bet you're really good at shooting baskets."

He knew a challenge when he heard one. "You think I can't?" he asked her.

Maggie just shrugged.

"Okay, smart guy, watch this." Buddy trotted over to the bleachers and retrieved the ball, dribbling it expertly back to the foul line. "Do you know anything about basketball?" Buddy asked Maggie.

"You throw it, and it goes through the hoop," Maggie replied.

"There's a lot more to it than that," Buddy explained patiently. "When you take a foul shot or a free throw, you have to set yourself exactly right."

"*Really?*" Maggie asked, wide-eyed with innocence.

"It's very scientific," Buddy continued. "Now just watch carefully." He dribbled the ball on the floor a few times, then gripped it tightly between both hands. He fixed his eyes on the net and went into a crouch.

There was a sudden rending sound.

"What was that?" Buddy demanded, his concentration momentarily broken, looking around for the source.

Maggie, Tad, and Kurt tried to cover their smiles.

"I think it was a janitor," Kurt answered.

"Go on, Uncle Buddy," Maggie urged. "Make a basket."

Buddy shot—a perfect swish. He straightened up and gazed at Maggie triumphantly. "Nothing to it," he said with false humility. "Now if you'll excuse us, we have an important meeting with the board of directors. Kurt."

"See you later," Kurt said to his son and gave Maggie a wink. He hurried to catch up with Buddy who was striding across the court, likening himself to Jerry West after a winning game.

Tad and Maggie let their smiles burst and began to laugh heartily.

Buddy had no way of knowing that he'd split his suit up the back.

SIXTEEN

IT WAS LATE WHEN MAGGIE GOT OFF THE ELEVATOR and struggled down the corridor with an armload of dress boxes. Tonight was Celia's night off, and Maggie had offered to fix dinner herself. But here it was after seven and Maggie was only now fumbling with her keys and unlocking the front door. She nudged it open with her knee and lurched into the foyer.

"Buddy?" she called into the apartment. It was dark —a good sign. Maybe he'd gotten tied up at the office and was going to be late. "Buddy?" she called again. "I got some great maternity dresses. I can even take them in after the big event."

No response. Maggie sagged with relief. She'd have time to whip something up after all. She had set the boxes down and started toward the hall when a sudden, unexpected sound stopped her in her tracks.

Giggling.

Someone was gigging in Buddy's bedroom. And that someone was unmistakably a woman.

Maggie stood perfectly still and listened. Maybe she'd imagined it. No. There it was again. And close behind it was Buddy's hearty chuckle.

Maggie peered down the dark hall and noticed a crack of light at the base of Buddy's door. She also became aware of the romantic Sinatra song that was filtering out of the stereo speakers in the living room.

Impulsively, Maggie tiptoed into the living room, slipped "The Love Sounds of the Great Sperm Whale" out of its record jacket, and stacked it on the spindle above the Sinatra disc.

She threw the reject switch.

The apartment went silent as the new record dropped into place. Maggie turned the volume knob as high as it would go, then stood back and covered her ears.

What came out of the speakers nearly blew the building apart—the Great Sperm Whale's mating bellow magnified a thousandfold. From Buddy's bedroom came a woman's scream of absolute terror.

Maggie chuckled.

Buddy, struggling into a bathrobe, charged into the living room like an angered elephant. "What the hell is going on?" he shouted above the ever-increasing din.

"They're playing our song!" Maggie shouted back.

Then she turned and defiantly strode past him into the hall where she passed an attractive redhead who, still terrified, was clutching a blanket to her nakedness.

Buddy walked over and switched off the stereo. The only sound was that of Maggie's door slamming down the hall.

"Who *was* that?" the redhead asked as she came into the living room.

"Nobody," Buddy replied, sounding confused and troubled.

For a full thirty seconds, he just stood there without moving or speaking, trying to get a handle on what the hell was going on with Maggie. She'd been acting very peculiar lately. Were all women like that during the fifth month? He'd have to look that up.

The next day, which was Saturday, Buddy decided that what Maggie really needed was to get out of the apartment and breathe some fresh air. So he took her along to Central Park where he was playing softball with the guys. They were a half-assed bunch, professional men who used the weekly game as an excuse to get a little exercise, blow off some steam, and consume large quantities of beer and junk food.

It never occurred to Buddy that Maggie would hit it off so well with his pals. He figured she'd probably just sit off to one side by herself under a tree or something and quietly watch. But not Maggie. Lately she'd begun to feel like some kind of princess in an ivory tower, and now she was going to make the most of being let out of her cage.

The boys went absolutely ape over her and insisted that she sit with them on the bench. Bunch of horny bastards, Buddy thought to himself. Put a pretty face in front of them, and they trip all over each other to see who can act like the biggest idiot.

But something else nagged at Buddy as he watched Maggie charm his friends. He began to wonder if he might not be just a little bit jealous.

By the bottom of the ninth, Buddy's team was up at bat and lagging behind on the scoreboard. If you'd asked Buddy the reason why, he might point out that his usually competitive teammates were more interested in Maggie than the game.

Larry, after striking out at bat, slid onto the bench beside Buddy.

"Nice try," Buddy told him without much enthusiasm.

Larry noticed that Buddy was watching Maggie out of the corner of his eye. She was farther down the bench, trading dirty jokes with a corporation vice-president and a magazine executive.

"There's something very special about that girl," Larry observed. "Very special."

Buddy ignored him and returned his attention to the

game at hand. "Come on, Jerry!" he shouted to the batter, trying to sound like his heart was in it. "This guy can't throw!"

"Don't you think she's special?" Kurt asked.

"Yeah, okay, she's special," Buddy agreed reluctantly. "Look at her down there with Nate and Tommy. I can tell you exactly what's on *their* minds."

"So what's it to you?" Larry asked.

"They're married men."

"Nate just got divorced."

"Nate's a jerk." Then Buddy turned back to the game. "Come on, Jerry! Knock it to Queens!"

"Buddy," Larry said, "I don't think you fully understand the emotions that can enter into a situation like this."

Buddy turned and gave him an incredulous look. "With two on and one out at the bottom of the ninth? Who *wouldn't* understand?"

Buddy turned back to the game. Larry smiled and shook his head. He knew that Buddy was purposely misunderstanding him.

Kurt the team captain walked over, looking worried. Then something occurred to him and his face brightened. "I'm putting her in," he announced.

"Putting who in?" Buddy asked.

"Maggie."

Before Buddy could react, Kurt formed a megaphone with his hands and called down to the bunch, "Hey, Maggie, you're up!"

Maggie paused in mid-joke and turned.

"You're up!" Kurt yelled. "Go in there and hit!"

For a moment, Maggie looked nearly as surprised as Buddy. Then she grinned happily and jumped to her feet as the men around her cheered their approval of Kurt's decision.

"Hey," Buddy said to Kurt, tugging at his sleeve, "*I'm* supposed to be up next. It's the last inning. We're behind."

Kurt gave him an evil grin. "You're O for Four."

"But I'm *due*," Buddy protested.

Larry gave Buddy a nudge in the ribs. "Give her a chance," he whispered. "Everybody wants her to play. Just look."

Sure enough. The team was cheering and clapping wholeheartedly as Maggie strode fearlessly to the batter's box.

"But it's *my* turn," Buddy repeated under his breath.

Maggie selected a bat. A player on the other team yelled, "You want a soft one or a hard one?"

Buddy jumped up off the bench. "Show a little respect, will you? That's a mother standing there!" Then unable to contain himself, Buddy ran around behind the backstop to get as close to Maggie as possible.

Maggie was really getting into it. She hefted the bat and took her stance beside home plate. She looked as cool and confident as any pro.

"Hey, Maggie," Buddy hissed to her, "get your shoulder up."

Maggie turned to give him a dirty look, but as she did, the pitcher let loose. The ball whizzed past her and smacked into the catcher's glove before she even knew what was going on.

"Strike one!" yelled the umpire.

"Hey, Buddy," shouted Larry. "Shut up!"

Seething with anger, Maggie turned back to face the pitcher. She gripped the bat hard, raised it off her shoulder, and concentrated. The pitcher began his windup.

"Keep your eye on the ball," Buddy whispered.

Maggie clenched her eyes shut in irritation. They were closed just long enough for the pitcher to get the ball off. It went right past her again.

"Strike two!" yelled the umpire.

Maggie swore under her breath. Buddy had thrown her off again.

Fortunately by this time, Kurt and Larry had run

over to Buddy behind the backstop and were telling him to keep his big mouth shut. Buddy argued that he had an investment to protect. They argued back that if he didn't keep quiet, they were going to let the whole team beat the shit out of him.

Maggie dug in at the plate. A hush fell over the field. This was it. Two strikes. One more and the game would be over. And Maggie's team would lose.

No one spoke a word. No one moved. Every eye was riveted on the pregnant woman at bat.

Dramatically, Maggie raised her arm and pointed to left field. Her teammates roared with enthusiasm. The courage of this girl! Buddy rolled his eyes heavenward.

Silence returned to the field as Maggie set herself. The pitcher went into his windup. Maggie grit her teeth and narrowed her eyes. The pitcher let loose with the ball. Maggie took a step into it and swung the bat with all her might.

Crack!

Buddy couldn't believe his eyes. She'd hit a fly ball. A *long* fly ball. The damn thing was disappearing into the sky above the left fielder's head—just as she'd called it! A cheer went up as Maggie dropped the bat and streaked toward first.

Buddy shouted above the cheering, "Slow down, Maggie! Take it easy!"

Maggie couldn't hear him. Not that it would've made a bit of difference even if she could. She rounded second and headed for third. By this time, though, the left fielder had caught up with the rolling softball and seized it in his hand.

"Stop at third!" Buddy screamed, but he knew it was useless.

Maggie turned the corner at third and headed in as the fielder heaved the ball toward home. He had a good arm, and it looked to Buddy as if Maggie would never beat the throw.

"Slide, Maggie!" yelled her teammates." "Slide!"

"No!" Buddy cried out and gripped the mesh of the backstop with his fingers. "Whatever you do, don't slide!!"

Maggie slid.

Buddy clamped his hands over his eyes and began to sink to his knees. He couldn't bare to look. The roaring filled his ears, and for a moment he thought he was passing out. But he wasn't passing out. The roar was the sound of his teammates as they ran onto the field to congratulate the heroine of the game. Maggie had made it—a home run!

Buddy lowered his hands and opened his eyes. Maggie was being holsted up on the shoulders of several guys. Everybody was laughing and cheering. Even the *other* team. Larry and Kurt had left Buddy's side and joined in the merriment. Maggie was paraded around and around the field.

"Don't drop her," Buddy said, but not very loud. He knew he couldn't be heard.

At long last Maggie was lowered to the ground and swept along with the tide to the coolers and picnic baskets where the guys broke out the food and drink.

Buddy watched the celebration from the sidelines, feeling foolish and left out. Normally he'd be right in there with the rest of them, popping beers, wolfing down hot dogs and chips. It's all Maggie's fault, he said to himself. I never should have brought her along. But Buddy knew this was just a ridiculous rationalization. He'd made an ass out of himself totally on his own.

He decided to take a little walk and get himself together. But as Buddy turned his back on the field, a sharp clear voice sang out above the others behind him.

"Oh, Buddy . . ." It was a taunting, tempting voice.

He turned in the direction of the voice, and his eyes nearly fell out of his head. He saw Maggie a few yards away, doing the unthinkable. The inconceivable. The impossible. She had grabbed a can of beer from one of the coolers and was defiantly popping the tab.

Horrified, Buddy opened his mouth and tried to speak, but his vocal cords were frozen. He staggered a few steps toward her and stopped, gaping with disbelief as Maggie lifted the can to her mouth and downed about half of it.

Buddy managed a strangulated scream. "Put that beer down," he ordered. "Not another sip, Maggie."

Her response to his command was to bend down, reach into one of the picnic baskets, and pull out a cellophane-wrapped Twinkie.

It was like waving a red flag in front of a bull. Wasting not a second, Buddy charged with hands outstretched to grab the offending Twinkie from her. Laughing, Maggie dodged him. Holding the beer in one hand and the Twinkie in the other, she took off running.

"Maggie!" Buddy shouted as he chased her across the baseball diamond. "Come back here!"

As if complying, Maggie stopped abruptly in the middle of center field and whirled around to face him. She closed a thumb over the top of the beer can and shook it. Just as Buddy was nearly upon her, Maggie removed her thumb and sprayed beer foam into his face.

"All right, cut it out." Buddy lurched around like a blind man. "Stop it, Maggie. This is juvenile."

"I know." Maggie laughed with delight. "It's juvenile and it feels terrific!"

She took off running again, exhilarated by her sudden mutiny. Buddy wiped the foam from his face and started after her again. Try as he might, he couldn't catch up with her. All that exercise he'd talked her into had paid off.

"Why are you doing this?" he shouted after her.

"Because I can't stand it anymore!" she yelled back,

enjoying her liberation. She slowed down slightly, knowing she could always pull out ahead of him if he got too close.

"*What* can't you stand?" Buddy was beginning to huff and puff. Maggie actually had to slow down even more to keep him within arguing distance.

"I'm sick and tired of *every*thing!" Maggie confessed. "The exercises, the diet, the noise you have piped into my room!"

"That's not noise!" Buddy had to dodge a couple of oncoming joggers. "That's the ocean!"

"Well, I don't want the ocean in my room!"

"It's called fetal relaxation, Maggie. Dr. Crassner says it's essential for the baby."

"Then have the baby with Dr. Crassner!" And in a gesture of defiance, Maggie threw aside the empty beer can and tore open the cellophane on the Twinkie. But before she could get it to her mouth, a roller skater suddenly whizzed into her path and brushed against her. The Twinkie tumbled out of her hand and into the dirt. Maggie almost stopped to retrieve it, but wisely decided to keep on running. Buddy purposely squashed the offending Twinkie underfoot as he made an effort to overtake her.

"This is against the spirit of the contract," he shouted desperately. His lungs were ready to burst. "Remember? You signed the contract. It's legally binding!"

"Screw the contract!" Maggie suddenly stopped alongside a little Greek vendor and his falafel cart. She turned and waited as Buddy came shuffling up, near exhaustion. He was too weak to do anything more than lean against the falafel cart and try to catch his breath. He and Maggie regarded each other soberly. He could see from the look on her face that she was mad—really mad. She was a stick of dynamite just waiting for him to light her fuse.

The little vendor looked back and forth between their tense faces. He smiled. "You want a falafel?" he asked timidly. "Nice falafel?"

Maggie, keeping her eyes on Buddy, nodded affirmatively. "Yeah," she said. "Gimme *two*."

Fire danced in Buddy's eyes, but he managed to keep a grip on himself. "Maggie," he said as gently as possible, "don't do it."

"Two falafels," Maggie said to the vendor.

"Two falafel comin' up."

"Don't give them to her." Buddy shot the vendor a threatening look.

The vendor shrugged, unperturbed. "I see this all the time," he remarked. "The male domination syndrome. Tell you what I do. I give you *each* two falafel. That way everybody happy. Four bucks."

He wrapped one up and handed it to Maggie. Greedily, she snatched it from him.

"Don't you dare eat that," Buddy warned. "Think of my son if you won't think of yourself."

"I *am* thinking of myself." Maggie tore away the wrapper and sank her teeth into the falafel. Buddy winced.

"I'm warning you," he said between clenched teeth. "Not another bite."

"Is good?" the vendor asked.

"Is *great*," Maggie replied ecstatically. She took another big bite.

"I'll have your license taken away," Buddy barked at the vendor.

The vendor shrugged. "I ain't got no license."

"No license?" Buddy looked at Maggie in terror. "Put that falafel down. This guy doesn't have a license to sell food."

Maggie ignored him and kept eating.

Buddy sagged with defeat. "Why are you doing this to me?" he wailed. "What did I *do*?"

"Is obvious," explained the vendor. "Stems from need to rebel against authority. Very common."

"What're you? The falafel therapist?"

"Any fool can see."

"He's right," Maggie said with her mouth full. "I feel smothered."

Buddy's face tightened with suspicion. "Is there someone *else* in your life?"

"There's no one in my life!" Maggie retorted. "There's not even *me* in my life." She took a second falafel from the vendor and stalked down the dirt trail. Buddy just stood there and watched her disappear, unable to figure her out.

"You got a lot to learn about women," the vendor informed him. Then he added, "That be two dollar for falafel. Advice I give free."

Buddy frowned at the smiling little Greek, pulled two singles out of his jeans, and thrust them at him. Then he started down the trail after Maggie.

Buddy decided it might be a good idea to let her cool off. He was pretty steamed himself. Continuing the confrontation right now would only make matters worse. So instead of catching up to her, Buddy decided to stay in the background and follow her unobtrusively.

For the next half-hour, he followed Maggie as she strolled aimlessly about the park. She knew he was tailing her, and he knew she knew. She didn't mind.

Maggie walked at a leisurely clip, often stopping to look at things that caught her interest. Buddy hovered in the near distance, waiting patiently until she continued walking again. When he felt that the time was right—that she'd cooled down—he quickened his stride and gravitated alongside her. Both were feeling rather foolish about the way they'd behaved.

Maggie did not acknowledge his presence with a look. She was too embarrassed at the moment. However, she was the first to speak.

"Can I ask you a question, Buddy?"

"Sure."

"Did you ever play professional sports?"

"Why?"

"You seem to take them so seriously."

"I *wanted* to play pro sports," Buddy admitted after a slight hesitation. "But I wasn't quite good enough."

Maggie sneaked a look at him. His eyes were downcast. She could see from his expression that this was not the kind of admission he made very often. For the first time, Maggie was seeing a side of this man that he'd kept well-covered.

"A person knows when he's good enough," Buddy went on. "And I knew that I wasn't. Besides, you didn't exactly grow up to be a sports star in the family I came from. My father used to say I could be anything I wanted to be as long as I went to law school."

He turned and gave her a smile. Maggie was quick to recognize the sadness it masked. She wasn't sure she liked seeing this side of him. It was much easier to see him as some kind of iceberg. In the past few seconds, he'd actually begun to resemble a human being.

"Is that why you want a son?" she asked.

"To go to law school, you mean?"

"To be a sports star."

From the other side of the park came the faint sound of cheering. Probably another softball game somewhere. Buddy and Maggie stopped to listen. After a bit, the sound faded away.

"I know a lot of pro athletes," Buddy said. "I meet them all the time at the Garden. They tell me the sound of cheering is the most beautiful sound in the world. I heard some of it myself when I was in high school and college." He paused for a moment. He was talking easily, but Maggie knew this kind of conversation was difficult for him. "But . . . do you know what *I* think the most beautiful sound in the world is?"

Maggie shook her head no, afraid that speaking might break the fragile spell.

"When I hear a kid laughing, I want to tape it and play it every morning" Buddy said wistfully. "There's no sound in the world like a kid's laughter."

Maggie studied him. He was staring off at nothing in particular, lost in his thoughts.

"There's a playground near the apartment," Buddy continued after a moment. "Everyday I pass it on my way to the Garden, and sometimes I stop to watch the kids. There's this one little guy—you oughta see him. He rides his bike and does all sorts of things nobody's supposed to be able to do on a bike. I mean this kid totally defies the laws of physics. Rides too close to the ground, rides on top of walls, rides everywhere. And he never falls over. But do you know when he's finally going to fall over?"

Maggie shook her head no.

"The day he learns about gravity. The day some schmuck tells him about gravity. That's why I want a son. So I can be there when he learns about gravity."

A chill wind had come up. Buddy dug his bare hands into his jeans pockets. He looked into the sky and watched a wedge of geese fly overhead.

Maggie bit her lower lip. She knew that things might get even worse now. It had been easier to regard him as an insensitive bastard who was exploiting her for his own selfish gain. Now she wasn't so sure, damn him. Just when she was getting comfortable resenting him.

Buddy turned to her. "Come on," he said, gently taking her by the elbow. "We'd better get home. It looks like rain."

Maggie could feel something growing inside her—and it wasn't the baby.

SEVENTEEN

BUDDY TUCKED THE PACKAGE UNDER HIS ARM AND pushed through the revolving doors to Thirty-fourth Street. He knew it would be some time before the kid could actually *use* a fielder's mitt, but it was always best to be prepared. He started down the sidewalk toward the Garden when a voice called out from behind, "Buddy!"

He stopped and turned around as a woman hurried up to him. She was an attractive woman in her early forties, and there was something familiar about her . . .

"Marilyn," he said suddenly. It had taken him a few seconds to comprehend that this woman was his ex-wife whom he hadn't seen in years.

"I thought I recognized you," she said with a trace of uneasiness in her voice. "I wasn't going to say anything at first, but I figure what the heck, let's be adults." She paused. "So whattaya say, Buddy? Let's be adults."

Buddy managed to smile. He was suddenly aware of butterflies in his stomach. "I thought you were living in Denver with what's his name . . . Herb."

"Herb?" She looked confused for a second. "Oh, *Herb*. Oh, no, I divorced him five years ago. I've remarried. I'm living up in Connecticut." Her rapid speech was betraying her own nervousness. "I just came into the city to see some girlfriends. You remember Sally and Claire."

Buddy nodded. He couldn't think of anything to say. Fortunately, Marilyn was willing to let him off the hook.

She indicated his package. "What's in the bag?" she asked.

Buddy looked down at the package and wondered what the hell was in it himself. Then he remembered. "This? It's a baseball glove. For my son."

Marilyn was taken by surprise. "Buddy, I had no idea you remarried."

"I'm not married," he replied and instantly wished he'd told her a lie.

"Oh. Divorced."

"Not divorced either." What the hell. Might as well tell her everything. She'll get a laugh out of it. "I hired a woman to have my baby."

Marilyn's jaw dropped. *"You?"* She couldn't believe what she was hearing. "Why would you hire somebody when there are women in this town just dying to marry you?"

"I didn't *want* to get married again."

The words stung her, and instantly he wished he could take them back. Marilyn looked away. She smiled sadly. "I really messed you up, didn't I?"

Buddy tried to soften the blow. "It was as much my fault as it was yours, Marilyn. We both wanted different things."

"And now you're getting what you want," she said softly, nodding at his package.

"How about you?" he asked. "Are you getting what *you* want?"

Marilyn suddenly looked at her watch. "Oh, no, I'm late for my luncheon." She leaned over and gave him a quick peck on the cheek. "I knew I'd run into you sometime. It was nice seeing you."

"You, too. Let's have lunch sometime," he offered.

"Real soon," she said and hurried to the curb to signal a taxi. One quickly drew up before her. She pulled open the back door and turned back to him.

"Bye, Buddy."

"Bye, Marilyn."

And then she was gone. Buddy stood on the sidewalk and watched the cab being swallowed up in traffic. He knew what she knew. There'd be no lunch.

Buddy adjusted the mitt under his arm and slowly walked away. He took stock of himself and concluded that Marilyn no longer meant anything to him.

He'd walked nearly ten blocks before he realized that he was going in the wrong direction.

EIGHTEEN

THE CAB PULLED UP IN FRONT OF AN OLD BROWNSTONE building. A cardboard sign taped to the entrance door identified it as "The School For Now." In the backseat of the cab, Buddy turned to his date, an attractive blond. "Look, Patti," he explained hurriedly, "I'm sorry, but this'll only take a minute."

"Hurry back," she sighed. This girl really knew how to say "hurry back." "I'm starving," she added.

Buddy grasped the door handle and was about to give it a yank when he suddenly felt something on his thigh—Patti's hand.

"Wait a minute," she pouted. "Aren't you going to give me a goodbye kiss?"

What an airhead! Buddy thought to himself. Not much upstairs but a real looker. He smiled and compliantly moved his mouth to hers. She nearly sucked his face in. Buddy had to struggle to work himself free.

"Plenty of time for that," he promised, his voice cracking. "But if we keep this up, I'm afraid the cabbie's going to have a coronary."

The driver quickly averted his eyes from the rearview mirror and pretended to be examining his fingernails.

"I'll be right back," Buddy assured her and abandoned ship.

As he hurried up the front steps, Buddy pulled a slip of paper out of his pocket and reread it. It was a short note in Maggie's scrawl—"Buddy, School for Now, 8:30 P.M., Room 16. Be there." Nothing else. He'd found it tacked to the refrigerator when he'd gotten home. No accompanying explanation. Just like Maggie, he thought to himself. Here he was with an honest to God *Vogue* model, and Maggie has to throw a crimp into the evening with a note that might either concern an emergency or nothing at all.

The front door was open, and the halls were empty. The classrooms looked dark. Buddy's steps echoed along the corridor as he rounded the first corner. Room 12. Room 13. Sixteen should be just around the next bend.

Maggie and Larry sat cross-legged on the floor in the dim light with twenty other couples. Everyone sat rigidly with eyes shut.

In the center of the room in a similar position, Dr. Muriel Shelby spoke in soothing tones. "Tonight," she was saying, "we'll learn how to breathe together. Just a little at first . . . talking and breathing . . ."

At which point the door opened and Buddy stumbled into the darkened room.

"Maggie?" he stage-whispered. "You here, Maggie?"

Buddy flicked on the switch, illuminating the room and twenty blinking, squatting couples.

"Sorry," he apologized nervously, "I was just looking for . . ." He spotted Maggie and Larry signaling to him from across the room. "There they are. Sorry. I'll just turn these back off . . ."

He cut the lights and started across the room before his eyes had a chance to adjust to the dark. A woman yelped as he accidentally stepped on her hand.

"Sorry," he said and weaved around Dr. Shelby who was observing him with undisguised irritation.

"May I ask who you are?" she inquired.

"Me?" Buddy replied. "I'm with that couple in the corner." He reached Maggie and Larry.

By now the whole group was staring—and glaring—at him. Buddy felt their eyes upon him and reddened with embarrassment. Fortunately it was pretty dark in there.

"Please continue," he addressed the gathering. "Pretend I'm not even here." He bent down and whispered to Maggie and Larry, "What the hell *is* this? It looks weird to me."

"We have a very delicate atmosphere here, sir," Dr. Shelby said somewhat harshly. "And now because of you, we'll have to start it over again."

Buddy nudged Larry. "What're *you* doing here?"

"Maggie called me."

"Yeah," Maggie added. "After you didn't show up. But now that you're here, you can get into the Indian position with the rest of us and stop holding up the class."

Buddy frowned, remembering Patti. "I don't think I can. You see—"

"We're *waiting*," Dr. Shelby addressed Buddy. The entire room was indeed waiting.

"It's important for the father to participate in this," Larry told Buddy.

"I've been coming to these for five months," Maggie said, trying to keep her voice down. "Now it's *your* turn."

Buddy shook his head. "I can't. I've got a slight problem."

"Yoo-Hoo. Buddy?"

Buddy's slight problem was standing in the open doorway, letting in light from the hall. "I'm ravenous," she said and looked around. "Hey, what *is* this?"

"Who are *you*?" Dr. Shelby demanded.

"I'm with *him*," Patti pointed to the guilty party across the room.

Dr. Shelby looked across the room at Buddy. "Is this young lady your wife?" she asked.

"No," Buddy replied weakly. He felt like he was in third grade, addressing the teacher. "I'm not married."

Dr. Shelby looked confused. "Then who's *she*?" she indicated Maggie this time.

"I'm the mother of his child," Maggie piped up.

"And I'm his date," Patti added.

Dr. Shelby raised an eyebrow and fixed Larry with a look. She was afraid to ask who *he* was.

"I'm just a friend of the family," Larry explained, enjoying the confusion.

Buddy leaned in close to Larry. What he was about to say was going to hurt, but it had to be done. "Have you ever been out with a *Vogue* model?" he whispered.

Larry grinned. "Not in *this* life," he replied.

"She's all yours," Buddy told him, indicating Patti, who was still standing in the doorway, high cheekbones and all. "Make up some story for me. You're a doctor. You're good at lying."

"Leave it to me," Larry assured him. He pulled himself up off the floor and made a beeline across the room.

"Okay," Buddy signaled to Dr. Shelby. "You can pick up where you left off."

"Thank you so much," she said icily.

Larry took Patti by the arm and steered her out. Buddy sighed inwardly. Fatherhood is full of such sacrifices, he told himself.

"Quiet," Dr. Shelby ordered.

The class settled down again, and Buddy, upon Maggie's insistence, reluctantly got himself into the Indian position. He found it nearly as painful as giving up Patti for the evening.

"We must all close our eyes and recreate an atmosphere again," Dr. Shelby instructed.

The class closed their eyes and began to recreate an atmosphere. Buddy felt silly.

"Now hold your partner's hand and just listen to the breathing of one another."

Maggie slipped her hand into Buddy's.

"Is she serious?" Buddy whispered.

"It's the method," Maggie replied.

"*What* method?"

"It was your goddamn idea, pal. You're the one who read her book and had me sign up for this."

"*She* wrote a book?"

"Now, *fathers*," Dr. Shelby was saying, "look into your wives' eyes and say, 'We are three.' "

"How much am I paying for this?" Buddy asked Maggie.

"We are three," said the men in the room—all the men but Buddy.

Dr. Shelby opened her eyes and looked over at Buddy. "I don't believe I heard *you*," she said.

"Say it," Maggie urged.

"I can't say that," Buddy replied, feeling put on the spot and uncomfortable. "It's silly."

"You have to," Maggie informed him.

A shadow fell over Buddy. He looked up and discovered Dr. Shelby towering over him. She did not look pleased. It was obvious that the class was not going to continue until Buddy said the words.

"All right," Buddy mumbled. "We are three."

"Louder please," said Dr. Shelby.

"Come on, Buddy," Maggie prodded, smiling at him.

Buddy swallowed. This kind of thing was not easy for him. "We are three," he said a little bit louder.

Satisfied, Dr. Shelby returned to her space. Buddy looked at Maggie, and she winked at him. He smiled back. "We are three," he whispered to her. He found himself rather enjoying the words.

"We are three," he said again.

NINETEEN

THE DINNER WAS MAGGIE'S WAY OF CALLING WHAT SHE hoped might be a permanent truce to the war she and Buddy had been subconsciously engaged in from the very beginning.

She'd planned it for days, shopped for it herself, had even planned to fix it herself. But when it came to cooking, Maggie was plain terrible, and so, desperately, she beseeched Celia to do it for her. Celia agreed warily, but not because she minded cooking. She didn't. She was wary because she liked Maggie and feared that the girl was setting herself up for a fall.

Celia's concern was well-founded.

It took Maggie nearly an hour to set the dining room table, but when she finished, it was truly a work of art. With the candles lit, it looked just like a television commercial for Harvey's Bristol Cream.

Maggie came into the kitchen to see how the cooking was coming along.

"Comin' along fine," Celia told her.

"This is really wonderful of you," Maggie said with rising excitement in her voice. "I'm such a lousy cook, and I want everything to be just right."

"If you ask me, you're just wastin' your time."

"It's only dinner," Maggie said innocently. "I'm calling a truce."

Celia turned from the sink and looked at her. Maggie tried to keep the oh-tonight-is-nothing expression fixed on her face to withstand Celia's scrutiny. "I know what to call it," Celia said. "You're fallin' for the guy."

Maggie laughed. "*Me?* Fall for *him*? You've got to be kidding, Celia. How could anybody fall for Buddy?"

Celia's brow furrowed. "I been tryin' to figure that out myself," she said. "Especially a smart girl like you."

Maggie shook her head. "I think you're jumping to the wrong conclusion. There's nothing about Buddy to fall for. He's rude, egotistical, selfish. We have no respect for each other, and we fight all the time."

"Sounds like you're already married," Celia observed.

"It's crazy. Me fall for Buddy. Ha."

"You're a good-looking girl," Celia said. "What's wrong with men your own age?"

"They're all too young."

Celia went back to slicing cucumbers. "Maggie, I gotta say it. I think you're askin' for trouble."

Maggie leaned against the counter. For nearly a minute she remained silent. Celia could tell she was forming an important question in her mind.

Finally Maggie turned to Celia. "What do *you* think of him?" she asked. "What do you *really* think of Buddy?"

Celia set the knife down. "I love him," she admitted, then hastily added, "only don't ever tell him that!"

Maggie sat down at the kitchen table. "Well," she announced, "I certainly don't *love* him."

Celia rested a hand on Maggie's shoulder. "Now all you gotta do is take that roast out in one hour," she said. "As for me, I'm gonna get outa here while the gettin' is good."

Maggie brought her own hand up and laid it on Celia's. "Thanks, Celia. I really appreciate your help."

"Don't thank me," Celia untied her apron and hung it on the pantry doorknob. "I just hope I ain't contributin' to somethin' that's gonna blow up in your face."

"I've planned out every detail," Maggie said with a confident smile. "Everything's going to be just fine."

Dressing took nearly an hour and a half, but the end result was well worth the trouble. Maggie had to admit it. She looked terrific. Pregnant, yes, but still terrific.

Carefully she lit the dining room candles and clicked off the overhead light. The walls of the room danced with warm, flickering light, and everything was bathed in a romantic orange glow. Perfect. Absolutely perfect.

A key turned in the front door lock.

Maggie flashed a quick look at herself in the mirror, smoothed her dress, and stood perfectly still alongside the dining room table. She'd wait right there until Buddy came through and discovered her. She could just imagine the look on his face.

The front door was opening . . . she could hear it . . . he'd be stepping in just about now . . . and now he'll probably call out, "I'm home," like he always does . . .

"How about a drink?" she heard his voice asking.

"I'd love one," replied a female voice.

The smile on Maggie's face disappeared as she was seized by sudden panic. Panic and anger. She felt like the world's biggest chump. Desperately, she blew out the candles on the table and flattened herself against the wall. Through the archway to the living room, she could see Buddy entering with a stunning, dark-haired woman who appeared to be everything Maggie was not —that is to say, she was not pregnant.

"I'll get a couple of glasses," Buddy said. "Sit down and make yourself comfortable."

He's coming this way! Maggie realized. Her impulse was to run, but she knew it was pointless. She'd have to face the music. As Buddy came through the archway, she stepped out in front of him.

"Maggie," he said in surprise. She looked like some kind of well-dressed burglar there in the dark room. "What are *you* doing home?"

"Gestating," was her weak response.

"This is your night at the clinic," he said with a trace of irritation.

"It was canceled." Maggie wanted to hit him with a chair.

"Why's it so dark in here?"

"I *like* it dark," she replied and managed to get herself between Buddy and the lightswitch. "The dark is supposed to be good for me. Some things grow better in the dark, you know. Like mushrooms."

"I don't want a mushroom, I want a baby," Buddy told her, then leaned in close to whisper. "Listen, that's Sophia Thatcher out there, the Houston society lady. Really a class act."

"You act like you're in love with her."

"I'm not in love with anybody," Buddy replied "But I am pretty crazy about Sophia. I always have been. So look, don't let on about our arrangement. In fact, I'd appreciate it if you'd make yourself scarce."

Maggie could feel the anger boiling up inside her. "Oh, don't worry," she assured him through clenched teeth. "I wouldn't dream of embarrassing you."

"Good girl." He gave her a pat on the arm and hustled back into the living room.

Sophia, who had heard voices but nothing that she could make out, looked up from the couch and smiled at him. She was forty or thereabouts but looked twenty years younger—and she had a smile that haunted Buddy for weeks everytime he'd seen her on her infrequent forays into New York. She was a remarkable woman, and she often made Buddy feel things he'd felt with no other woman.

Maggie peeked at her from the dining room. Sophia was something to look at all right. And just look at

Buddy, the big dumb ass, fawning all over her. Maggie made up her mind.

"Well," Buddy was saying to Sophia, "all the glasses are dirty. Why don't we blow this pop stand and have a drink out someplace? Then we can go on to dinner."

"Sounds like a plan," Sophia replied.

At that moment, Maggie came fluttering out of the kitchen, wearing Celia's apron around her waist and— of all things—an old plastic margarine dish atop her head like a maid's cap. She was all smiles.

"Hello there," she said to Sophia.

Sophia smiled back but looked puzzled. It occurred to her that maybe this was a demented sister Buddy kept locked up in the apartment.

"Why, Maggie." Buddy stumbled nervously for an explanation. "Uh . . . Sophia . . . I'd like you to meet . . . my . . . my . . ."

"His *au pair*," Maggie said with a smile and a curtsy.

"Right. My *au pair*." Buddy took Sophia by the hand, guiding her off the couch and toward the front door. "Good night, Maggie."

Sophia disengaged herself and turned back to Maggie. "You're going to be a mother soon, aren't you?" she asked with genuine interest.

"Not soon enough," Maggie answered sweetly, shooting daggers at Buddy.

"Maggie," said Buddy, giving her a dirty look of his own behind Sophia's back, "why don't you take the night off?"

"Oh, may I?" Maggie feigned excitement. "Why, Mr. Evans sir, that's so very kind of you." She curtsied her appreciation, and Buddy winced.

"Who's the proud father?" Sophia asked.

"There is no father," Buddy said and steered Sophia to the door.

"No father?" Sophia was confused. "A *virgin* birth?"

"Well, you know," Buddy chuckled nervously, "Maggie's a Catholic." He pulled the front door open and managed to get Sophia through it.

"I just love looking at pregnant women," Sophia confessed on the other side. "Don't you, Buddy?"

"Oh, God, yes," he replied and started to close the door behind them. He wasn't fast enough.

Maggie pushed through and into the hallway, shrugging on her overcoat.

"Where do you think *you're* going?" Buddy demanded.

"You gave me the night off," Maggie replied innocently. Then she turned to Sophia. "It was very nice to meet you. Good night," she stated as she pulled open the door to the stairway.

"But aren't you riding down in the elevator?" Sophia wanted to know.

Maggie regarded Buddy for a moment. He was holding his breath and looking scared. Good. Just the way she wanted him. "I'm afraid I have to use the service stairs," she explained, hanging her head forlornly.

"That's silly and dangerous," Sophia protested. She took Maggie by the arm and escorted her to the elevator. "You'll ride down with us, Maggie."

"That's so kind of you," Maggie said, flashing a sneaky grin at Buddy who had suddenly gone white with fear. He grimaced and punched the down button—extra hard.

"So who's the father?" Sophia asked again while they waited for the elevator to arrive.

"Aren't elevators wonderful things?" Buddy suddenly asked before Maggie had a chance to reply. "Can you imagine how long it would take us to walk down all those stairs? Boy, we'd really be tired, wouldn't we?"

Fortunately for him, the elevator doors parted at that moment, and the three of them stepped inside. Buddy hit the lobby button—again extra hard for he had to take it out on something—and leaned his back against the wall of the elevator car, praying silently to himself that Maggie would have the good sense to knock off her little game.

His prayers were not answered.

"You want to know about the father?" Maggie inquired of Sophia.

"Hey, look at this!" Buddy pointed to the framed inspection card on the wall. "Inspected by Thomas Kroger. Wait a minute—not *Tommy* Kroger! You're kidding me. Sophia, look at this. Tommy Kroger inspects the elevators at the *Garden*. Everytime you step into an elevator, there's his name. Son of a gun!"

"I was raped," said Maggie.

Sophia's dark eyes widened with horror. Buddy continued, "That Tommy Kroger sure gets around. I'll bet he even—*rape?!* Are you crazy?" He turned on Maggie like some kind of madman. "You weren't raped."

"Yes, I was."

Buddy got a handle on himself and chuckled nervously to Sophia, who was beginning to eye him with suspicion. "The father was *killed*," he explained.

"Killed?" Sophia repeated.

"Killed," Buddy declared. "In . . . in the war."

"What war?"

"The big one. The big war. The . . . oh, for Chrissake. Details. Who cares what war as long as he's dead? That's the important thing."

Sophia put a consoling hand on Maggie's shoulder. "I'm sorry I brought it up, Maggie. War is a terrible thing. It must be very painful for you."

Maggie nodded. Then without warning, she suddenly burst out crying. It was a difficult stunt to pull off when your true impulse was to explode with laughter.

"She'll get over it," Buddy told Sophia. "Look at the Japanese."

The elevator doors opened, and Buddy stepped out,

hoping Sophia would stick with him. He should have known better. Sophia placed a sympathetic arm around Maggie and led her through the lobby, apologizing all the way for having brought up so many painful memories.

Outside on the street, Buddy told the doorman to forget the cab, they'd walk. Then he tried, without any success, to pry Sophia off Maggie who's crying had reached Academy Award nomination proportions.

"Poor Maggie," Sophia was sharing her pain. "Do you want to talk about it? Sometimes it helps."

"I think she needs to be alone," Buddy suggested.

"He *wasn't* killed," Maggie sobbed. And suddenly what had begun as a joke turned into reality. Maggie was *really* crying now. All the frustration and all the disappointment of the past days had finally found vent. "He *wasn't* killed," she repeated over and over, her body shaking as the tears ran down her cheeks.

Buddy stared at her. Even he could tell that she wasn't play-acting anymore. He felt terrible.

"Then what happened to him?" Sophia asked, cradling Maggie.

"I'm a . . . a . . ." Maggie suddenly blurted it out. "I'm a surrogate mother!"

"A *what?*" Sophia responded incredulously.

"Oh, God." Buddy looked for a car to throw himself in front of. The jig was up.

"A surrogate mother," Maggie repeated tearfully. "A man is paying me to have his child."

"No!" Sophia gasped and lifted a hand to her mouth. "Why—that's *barbaric!*"

"Well," Buddy managed weakly, "I don't know if I'd go *that* far."

Sophia turned to him. "Don't you believe in the sanctity of marriage?"

"Of course I do," Buddy sputtered back. "Matrimony is what keeps most marriages together."

"You're not going to be alone tonight," Sophia comforted Maggie. "You're coming along with us."

"Oh, I couldn't do that," Maggie managed, then began sobbing all over again.

"Maybe she's right," Buddy added. "Maybe I should take her back to the apartment."

"Nonsense," said Sophia. "Maggie's coming with us. I won't take no for an answer."

Buddy's heart stopped beating for a moment. He could feel it—the beginning of the end was at hand.

TWENTY

A SHORT TIME LATER, THE THREE OF THEM WERE
encamped at an intimate table in a fashionably intimate
restaurant. The sobbing had subsided, but Maggie remained tearful. Sophia still held her hand, giving her
sisterly comfort and compassion. Buddy was wishing
he could wake up from the whole dumb nightmare.

"Maggie," Sophia was saying in sympathetic tones,
"you're nothing more than a slave. It's positively me-
dieval."

"I'm sure Maggie would like to talk about something
else," Buddy offered.

"No, I wouldn't," Maggie said. "You're right, Sophia.
I *am* nothing more than a slave."

Sophia shook her head in disgust. "What kind of a
man would do this?"

Buddy flipped open his menu. "How do you ladies
feel about asparagus?" he asked. "Personally I hate it.
Now broccoli, on the other hand—"

"Was he . . . *brutal*?" Sophia asked.

"No," Maggie replied softly. "He was actually very
. . . *gentle*."

Buddy reacted with surprise to her statement. "See?"
he said to Sophia. "He was gentle. Sounds like a
helluva nice guy to me. Shall we order?"

Sophia looked at Buddy and smiled warmly. Then she gave him a peck on the cheek. "Buddy, it was so good of you to take Maggie into your home."

He shifted uncomfortably in his seat. "It's the least I can do," he said, smiling weakly.

"That's the thing about this man," Sophia said, turning back to Maggie. "Most people think he's just a cold fish. But he's really a very warm, caring person."

Maggie nodded in agreement. "He's been like a father to me and my child."

"How about a salad?" asked Buddy. "Anybody for salad?"

"Maggie, come with me," Sophia said, standing up. "Let's go to the powder room and freshen you up."

The powder room?! Buddy was seized with fear. So far he'd managed to deflect the conversation and keep it away from specifics, but now he could feel the whole thing slipping out of his hands. Maggie stood up, dabbing her eyes with a napkin.

"We'll be right back," Sophia told Buddy.

Buddy opened his mouth to protest, but no sound emerged. He'd run out of sounds and run out of diversions. Sensing doom, he settled back in his chair and watched the two of them leave the dining area. Buddy finished off his Scotch and water. He had a sudden sensation of eyes upon him. Looking up, he discovered the waiter standing over his shoulder, poised with pen and pad.

"What're *you* staring at?" Buddy demanded.

"Excuse me, sir," the waiter apologized, "but would you care to order now?"

"Why the hell not?" Buddy figured. "I guess it's customary for the condemned man to have one last meal."

"*Sir?*"

"Forget it," Buddy said and proceeded to order the most expensive items on the menu. If you're going to go, he told himself, go big.

*　*　*

In the ladies room, Sophia placed Maggie in a straightback chair facing the mirror and then sat down in another one beside her. Their eyes met in the mirror, and they exchanged hopeful smiles.

"Do *you* have children?" Maggie asked.

"Oh, yeah. Three of 'em."

"Really?"

"Two boys and a girl," Sophia replied proudly. "They're in Texas with my ex-husband."

Maggie nodded. She found herself liking this woman enormously. She even felt a little guilty for having put her on earlier. "Did you gain a lot of weight when you were pregnant?" Maggie asked.

Sophia threw back her perfectly coiffed head and laughed heartily. "God," she said, "I couldn't even walk. I was as huge as a house."

Sophia's laughter was infectious. Maggie found herself laughing along. It was such a pleasure to talk privately with another woman like this. Especially after being shut up with Buddy for so long. Maggie found herself wanting to let out everything she'd bottled up for so long.

"I had a dream last night," Maggie confessed. "I dreamt I was the Port Authority building."

Sophia burst out laughing. "I know what you mean, honey," she said. "I used to have dreams like that myself."

Maggie couldn't stop talking now. She was so grateful to have someone she could relate to. "I feel everything it seems. In my body—everything. All sorts of tingles and twitches. I even think I can sometimes hear the blood running through my veins. Especially at night when I'm lying down. But sometimes," and here her voice lowered, "I get so frightened. I don't have anybody to talk to. I didn't really care about the child at first, but now . . . I really love him, Sophia." Maggie placed her hand on her swollen belly. "I just hope he turns out healthy."

"He will," Sophia assured her. "Let me tell you something. My first child, my oldest boy, was born with a very flat head. It looked very strange. I was so worried that something was wrong or that it would make things hard for him growing up. But the doctor told me not to worry. He told me that he was certain his head wouldn't stay like that. And do you know *why* he was so certain?"

"No. Why?"

"Because he said he'd never seen an *adult* with a head like that."

Both women burst out laughing. When the giggling subsided, Sophia reached over and laid her hand on Maggie's. Then she looked Maggie directly in the eye. "Buddy's the father," she stated knowingly, "isn't he?"

Maggie hesitated. She could tell from Sophia's expression that she knew the truth. Maggie gave in and nodded. "Yes," she admitted. "Buddy's the father."

"Are you in love with him?"

Maggie stared down at her hands. "I don't know," she answered. There was genuine confusion in her voice. "Sometimes . . . sometimes I think I am. Then I wonder if it isn't just because of the baby."

"Buddy's a tough nut to crack," Sophia said with affection in her voice. "But he's really a good man, Maggie. Underneath."

Sophia appraised Maggie's matronly reflection in the mirror. "Tell me," she said with a secret smile, "how do you like having big tits?"

Maggie's face brightened with amusement. "That's the best part," she laughed.

Buddy downed his third Scotch and water and closed his eyes. Twenty minutes they'd been gone. He could just imagine the conversation going on in there. Maggie tearfully blurting out all the gory details, Sophia lapping them up. The two of them agreeing on what a heartless bastard he was. One wall away and there was nothing he could do. The powder room. That bastion of female supremacy where no man dares to go.

A rustling sound startled him, and he opened his eyes just as Maggie slid onto the chair opposite him. She looked refreshed, happy even. Buddy didn't like the smile on her face.

"Where's Sophia?" he asked, looking around. A thought entered his mind. What if Maggie in a pique had taken Sophia to the ladies room and murdered her? The way Maggie'd been acting all evening, he wouldn't put it past her.

"Sophia's a terrific lady," Maggie remarked, digging into the Châteaubriand. "I like her a lot."

"Leave that stuff alone," Buddy ordered. "What did you do to her?"

"Nothing. She had to go."

"Go where?"

Maggie shrugged. "Home, I guess."

"Quit stuffing your face," Buddy commanded. "You told her, didn't you? You told her everything."

"This is good." Maggie indicated the food Buddy had ordered. "Why don't you try some before it gets cold?"

"You told her." Buddy lowered his face into his hands. "You told her all about our arrangement."

"She guessed it," Maggie said matter-of-factly. "Buddy, I want to ask you something important." Her face was a mask of seriousness. "What are you going to tell him about his mother?"

Buddy made an opening between the fingers covering his face and regarded her quizzically. "Tell *who*?"

"Your precious heir. Your son. What are you going to tell him happened to his mother?"

Buddy dropped his hands. It was the first time the question had occurred to him. He searched his mind for an answer. "I don't know," he finally replied. "Maybe he won't ask."

"He's gonna notice he doesn't have a mother."

"I'll tell him we were divorced," Buddy said brightly.

"And suppose he wants to meet me?"

"I'll stall him."

"All his life?"

"No, all *mine*." Buddy grinned at her. Maggie did not grin back. She saw nothing amusing in his response. She was serious about this—it had been on her mind for some time. "Okay," Buddy said. "I'll tell him you died."

Maggie threw her napkin down and stood up. She could take no more.

"Where do you think you're going?" Buddy wanted to know.

"As far away from you as I can get!" Maggie flung the words at him like a knife. Then she turned and stomped through the restaurant in the direction of the door.

"Wait a minute!" Buddy stood up and shouted after her, momentarily forgetting that he was in the middle of a crowded restaurant. "Where are you going with my child?"

The whole room fell silent; diners stopped in the middle of their conversations and looked up in surprise. Maggie hesitated at the door. "I'm going to practice my French with *our* child," she yelled back at him. "You hear me? *Our* child!"

"*Our* child?" Buddy was horrified. The day he'd dreaded had come. His biggest fear had suddenly come true. "Wait a minute, Maggie. That kid is *mine*."

"Possession is nine-tenths of the law!" she shouted back.

Aside from Buddy and Maggie, everyone in the dining room—the diners, the waiters, the busboys—were frozen. It was like one of those science fiction movies where time suddenly stands still.

"I don't need the law!" Buddy yelled trimphantly. "I've got a contract!"

"Screw the contract!" Maggie shouted angrily. "And screw you, too!" Her words echoed through the restaurant. Maggie turned and strode out.

Everyone turned to Buddy for his reaction. Her words had stunned him. He'd never seen her like this before. Why was she doing this *now?* A couple more weeks and the baby would be born—he'd have his son and she'd be winging her way to France. Slowly Buddy's eyes unglazed, and he began to focus on the stares of the people around him. It suddenly dawned on him. He was standing in the middle of a crowded restaurant, making an ass out of himself.

TWENTY-ONE

THE FRENCH INSTITUTE/ALLIANCE FRANÇAISE WAS located in a small brownstone on West Seventy-first Street. Buddy knew the address because he'd been writing tuition checks to the place for the past eight months.

After sticking his head into half a dozen classrooms without luck, Buddy finally came upon a large room identified as the language lab where a dozen or so students were enclosed in soundproof booths, responding in unison to the lesson that came to them over the earphones they wore. Buddy could barely make out their muted responses.

"What is playing at the movies tonight?" the students asked mechanically, then translated, *"Qu'est - ce - qu' on joue ce soir au cinema?"*

Buddy spotted Maggie in earphones hunched over her textbook in one of the glass booths. He tried its door. Locked. Next he tapped on the glass, but Maggie refused to acknowledge his presence. Either that or she couldn't hear him.

"Maggie," Buddy called, tapping louder. "We have to talk."

Maggie's eyes did not waver from her text. Buddy could see her lips moving, forming the proper replies. Looking around the room in frustration, Buddy spied the instructor at the far end, speaking into a microphone and conducting the lesson. At least *he* wasn't locked in a booth. Buddy made a beeline to the instructor's desk and tapped the young Frenchman on the shoulder.

"There's a phone call for you outside," Buddy lied urgently.

"For me?"

"Yeah." Buddy nodded emphatically. "Very urgent. A matter of life and death."

Looking worried and confused, the instructor hopped up and tore out of the room. Buddy slipped behind his desk and leaned in close to the microphone. "Maggie," he said desperately, "please listen to me."

"Maggie, please listen to me," repeated the class.

Maggie looked up in surprise and recognized Buddy behind the instructor's desk.

"You're acting like a jackass," he said.

"You're acting like a jackass," the class reiterated.

Maggie jumped up and yanked off her earphones. "Get away from me!" she yelled over the glass of her booth.

"We have a contract," Buddy insisted.

"We have a contract," the class echoed.

Maggie unlocked the door to her booth, pushed it aside, and ran right out of the room. Buddy pushed himself away from the microphone and gave chase.

He found her in an empty classroom across the hall, her arms folded defiantly across her chest and resting atop her jutting stomach. Her feet were planted, and she seemed ready for the oncoming confrontation. She looked so fierce that Buddy almost considered retreating.

"You and I made a deal," Buddy reminded her, trying to keep his voice calm. "A deal's a deal, Maggie."

"The deal stinks," she replied tightly.

"It doesn't matter whether you think it stinks or not. What you're doing is illegal."

"Have you made up your mind about what you're going to tell him about me?"

"Yes," Buddy nodded. "I'm going to tell him the truth."

"Which truth is that?"

Buddy narrowed his eyes at her. "I'm going to tell him that he was *cloned*."

Maggie shook with anger and tried to escape past him. Buddy caught her by the arm and held onto it. Maggie fought to free her arm and glared at him. Buddy was afraid she might actually spit in his eye. Or worse.

"You're insane, Buddy," she said. Her anger was beginning to dissipate, though. She was getting tired of being mad. It was hard work for a pregnant lady.

"Put yourself in my place." Buddy pleaded. "Will you do that? Will you just calm down and put yourself in my place?"

"All right," Maggie said and allowed herself to cool down. Buddy could see the tension leaving her face and body. "Okay," she said at last. "I'm in your place."

"And what do you think?"

"I think I'm insane!" she shouted, the anger rushing back.

Defeated, Buddy dropped into one of the wooden student desks. "Maggie," he said wearily, "I didn't want to become the villain in all this. I just wanted a son."

Maggie could see that she had him against the ropes. There was no sense in pushing him any further. She sat down in the little desk beside his. "What about love?" she asked.

"Love?" Buddy ran his finger over the grooves that delinquents had carved into his desk top. "Love has gone the way of the hoola-hoop and the ten-cent cup of coffee. I thought you looked at it that way, too."

Maggie didn't reply. He was right, of course. She *had*

looked at it that way for as long as she could remember. And now she didn't know *how* she felt; her feelings and emotions were all mixed up.

"You know what it's like," Buddy went on. "Men and women meet now, they develop a deep social and sexual longing for each other, they share each other's experiences, and they want to spend the rest of their lives together." He paused and looked over at her. "How can you call that love?" he asked.

Maggie didn't know how to answer.

Suddenly, without warning, a man and a woman rushed into the classroom, carrying a second woman who appeared to be in great pain.

"Put her down gently," the man said. His voice was thick with worry.

He and the first woman helped the second woman down to the floor where she stretched out, groaning. It was instantly apparent that she was pregnant, *very* pregnant.

"Do you mind?" Buddy asked them, noticing only that they had been interrupted. "We're trying to have a personal conversation here."

"Well, my wife is having a personal baby," the man replied.

"*A baby?!*" Buddy jumped up and stared at the woman on the floor. She was obviously going into labor.

"Phone Lenox Hill," the husband instructed the first woman. "Tell them we need a doctor immediately."

She nodded and ran out of the room. Maggie left her desk and hurried to the man's side. "Can I help?" she asked.

The man looked her up and down and noticed her own pregnant state. "You look like you might know something about this," he said.

"Only what I've learned in class," she replied, trying to stay calm. She was both thrilled and terrified at the same time.

The wife suddenly let out a cry of pain that froze Buddy's blood. He'd never heard anything like it before. It made *him* want to scream.

"This is my wife," explained the man. His face was ashen with concern. "I've helped her with three of them so I know a few of the tricks. However," he turned to Maggie, "this is going to be a real baptism of fire for *you,* Miss."

Buddy took a few nervous steps toward them. He felt that he might pass out at any second. "What do you want *me* to do?" he asked, his voice trembling.

The man looked up at Buddy's frightened face. "You stand in the corner," the man instructed.

Obediently, Buddy retreated to the far corner and watched from there. He could feel his heart pounding against his chest. This was it, the real thing, and he had a front-row seat.

The husband pulled a handkerchief out of his pocket and thrust it into Maggie's trembling hand. "Here. Wipe her forehead with it."

Maggie gently swabbed the woman's perspiring brow. The woman looked up at Maggie, her eyes glazed. "It happened like this before," the woman said. She sounded frightened.

"I'm Maggie. Don't worry—you're gonna be all right."

"I lost him," the woman told her. "I lost him the last time."

Maggie gulped. "Well, you're not gonna lose him this time," she promised. She reached over and gripped the woman's hand. "Everything'll be fine."

"Can you breathe?" the husband asked Maggie.

"Yes. I learned in class."

"Good. Help her breathe."

"I'm so scared," the woman clasped Maggie's hand and searched her face for reassurance.

"Don't you worry," Maggie said confidently—she

was actually beginning to *feel* confident. "There's nothing to be scared about."

The woman let out a scream and gripped Maggie's hand so tightly that Maggie almost let out a howl herself.

The husband bit his lower lip. "This one's not gonna wait any longer."

"Oh God," Buddy said to himself. He could not take his eyes away. He wished there was something he could do to help.

"Can you handle it?" the husband asked Maggie.

Maggie nodded. "I can handle it," she said.

And she did.

From his corner of the room, Buddy stood perfectly still and watched a miracle take place.

Buddy was having a difficult time making up his mind as to which was more beautiful, Maggie or the screaming infant she held in her arms, swaddled in the husband's jacket. She bent down and held the child close to its mother. The mother's face was nearly as blotchy and tear-stained at the baby's, but the smile on her face was something else. Something incredible.

"It's a girl," Maggie told the mother, her own voice swelling with emotion. "And she's fine—just fine."

"I'm going to call her Maggie," the woman replied, her voice barely audible. "After *you*, Maggie."

The tears Maggie had been holding back suddenly let loose and ran down her face. The exhausted husband gave her a kiss on the cheek. "You were a charm," he told her gratefully.

Buddy was slowly approaching from behind, trying to get a glimpse of the baby. He was grinning ecstatically, feeling that in his own way he had helped—helped by praying throughout the whole ordeal. Buddy wanted to hold it. "Can I . . ." he began to ask, but before he could get out another word, a team of paramedics rushed in with a stretcher, causing him to step out of the way.

"Lady, you got yourself one beautiful baby," said one of the paramedics as they gently placed the mother on the stretcher.

The mother looked at Maggie. "Will you come with me?" she asked.

"Sure," Maggie said, pleased. "I'd love to."

"Is this going to be your first?" the mother asked, indicating Maggie's stomach.

"Yeah," Maggie said, suddenly filled with pride. "It'll be my first."

"It'll be beautiful, too," the mother predicted.

Buddy felt happy but left out. He stood in the background as they carried the mother and baby out. Maggie went with them, all the while holding the mother's hand. One of the paramedics remained for a moment, jotting down information on a clipboard. Buddy moved to his side.

"Did you see what she did?" Buddy asked him, grinning proudly. "Did you see what that girl did? She was incredible. And she's gonna have my baby. That girl's gonna have my baby."

The paramedic smiled back at him, then left the room.

Buddy just stood there, all alone, smiling. "That girl is gonna have my baby," he repeated to no one.

TWENTY-TWO

BUDDY DECIDED TO DO SOME CELEBRATING. HE FIG-ured that Maggie wouldn't be home for a while so he took a cab from the French Institute to a favorite watering hole where he was sure to know a few of the patrons—or the bartender at any rate.

By the time he got home, it was well after midnight and the apartment was dark. Buddy staggered into the living room and flicked on a lamp. Maggie must be in bed by now, he figured. Better not wake her. He was anxious to apologize to her for his behavior, but thought it might be better to let her sleep and wait until morning.

He was just about to trudge off to bed when something on the coffee table caught his attention. Propped up against an ashtray was an envelope addressed to "Mr. Evans" in Maggie's unmistakable handwriting.

Buddy tore open the envelope and unfolded the letter inside. The message was simple and direct. "I am leaving and taking the child with me. Don't try to find me. I'm sorry this had to happen."

For the longest time, Buddy just stared at it. Then his hand began to shake. Then his whole body. Buddy dropped onto the couch and read the note over again. He shook his head—maybe it was the booze.

You've blown it, he thought. You had your chance, and you blew it by behaving like an idiot. Wishing he could have the day over again was pointless. Maggie was gone. The child was gone.

Still, this was a woman capable of anything. Who knew what lengths she'd be driven to in her desperation. Something had to be done. Someone had to think of his son's welfare.

"Now explain to me who was kidnapped, Mr. Evans?" The desk sergeant at the precinct house wasn't sure about the three guys who stood in front of him. The tallest and youngest of them seemed to be on some kind of drug. He was all nerves. The one who called himself a doctor obviously found the other fellow very amusing. And the third character, who claimed to be a lawyer, seemed more upset with his client than he was anxious to help him.

"My son," stated Buddy.

The sergeant began to take notes. "What's his name?"

Buddy froze for a moment, then blurted out. "Roger. No! I mean Geoffrey. Or Quinby. That's Scandinavian. A Scandinavian name."

The desk sergeant stared at Buddy. Larry was trying to keep back his laugh, and Kurt rolled his eyes, something he'd become very adept at doing these past nine months.

Buddy shot a killing glance at Larry and then smiled in the direction of the desk sergeant. "Let's call him Boy."

"Do you know who took him?"

Buddy thought. "The baby-sitter."

"Describe her."

"Rude. Egotistical. Selfish—"

"I think he means a physical description," interrupted Kurt.

"Oh. Physical. Let's see."

"What was her height, Mr. Evans?"

"Medium."

"Her weight?"

"Medium."

"Her hair?"

"Kind of . . . medium."

"No distinguishing characteristics," asked the sergeant.

Buddy thought for a second. "None. Do you need anything more specific?"

Larry walked toward a water fountain and started to laugh. The others stared at him. "Something in my throat. I'm okay." Kurt tried to get Buddy's attention.

"Buddy, look, why don't we go back to the apartment and talk about this?"

"No way. That girl kidnapped my son! I'm going to find her!"

The sergeant tried again. "Maybe if you'd describe your son, Mr. Evans."

Buddy gestured helplessly with his hands. "Well, he's, uh, he's . . . hard to describe actually."

"Is he tall? Short? What?"

"Actually, Sergeant, he's more round."

Larry couldn't hold it in any longer. He tried covering his laughter with phony coughing. This was classic.

The sergeant was losing his patience. "Just tell me when he was born."

Buddy looked to Kurt.

"Don't look at me, pal," said Kurt. "I can't help you. I'm only your lawyer."

Buddy leaned toward the desk sergeant. "It's kind of hard to pin down. You see there's a strange twist to this case that might interest you a lot as a criminal investigator." Buddy looked at Kurt. "Don't you think the sergeant will be fascinated by the details of this case?"

Kurt shook his head. "No."

Buddy waded forward. He spoke very slowly. "You see, Sergeant, my son isn't born yet." There was a long pause during which the sergeant counted the years left until his retirement.

"Strange, isn't it, Sergeant?"

The sergeant nodded.

Half a minute later, if you were traveling down the street just outside the precinct, you would have seen two men holding a third man. The third man was screaming and waving his arms. If you were close enough, you might be able to hear him say, "I'm not the goddamned criminal! *She* took my baby! I pay my taxes. They can't say things like that about me!"

TWENTY-THREE

Maggie trudged through the dark Soho streets, heading for the loft where she hoped Billy, Johnnie, and Phones would be practicing. Several things were on her mind. For starters, she'd just run away from Buddy and felt lost. She hoped the group would at least be kind enough to put up with her for a couple of days until she got her bearings straight. But as she approached the familiar facade of the loft building and heard the last few bars of an awful punk song coming from the floors above her, she realized that none of them had seen her pregnant before. Not *really* pregnant. Oh, well, there was no way around it this time.

Getting off the elevator, she noticed that the room was quiet. There were boxes and suitcases in a not-so-neat pile by the door. The three others were across the large room packing their instruments.

Billy and Johnnie were talking about travel plans.

"What about the TV?" asked Johnnie.

"They have TVs in Boston, Johnnie."

"They do?" Johnnie looked surprised. "Newspapers, too?" Obviously a true New Yorker. Maggie took a few steps toward them. Billy was the first to notice. He smiled. Then as his gaze traveled down to her protruding abdomen, his smile vanished. He looked up quickly to meet her eyes.

Maggie feigned nonchalance. "Hi, guys."

Phones waved from under her headset. Johnnie came trotting over to her.

"Hey, baby, how're you doing?" Johnnie kissed her. "We got a gig up in Boston. The group's been doing real well since . . . since you left."

"I've heard."

Billy walked up to her slowly and circled her. Johnnie didn't even seem to notice she was pregnant. Billy just shook his head. Maggie took a deep breath under this scrutiny.

"You're pregnant," said Billy in a low and disbelieving voice.

"I know." Maggie smiled.

Johnnie finally noticed. "Holy God! He's right! You're pregnant."

Billy regarded her. "How did it—?"

Phones was joining in by this time. She started to explain to Billy. "You see, this is how it happens—"

"I know how it happens!" shouted Billy. "What I meant was—"

Maggie cut him off. "Listen, before you say anything, I just wanted to know if I could crash here for a couple of nights. I won't get in your way, I promise."

Billy smiled at her. "Our place is yours. You know that."

Meanwhile, Buddy was driving along a country road in upstate New York slow enough to read the names on the mailboxes.

On the front seat next to him was a letter addressed to Maggie in care of his apartment. In the upper left-hand corner was the return address of a Lorraine Harden, Maggie's mother. Buddy had found the discarded letter while rummaging through Maggie's desk drawers in the hope of finding some clue to her whereabouts. The letter from her mother—which he hadn't read—was all he found. He decided not to call. He thought a personal visit was the best route to take.

So he spent the day driving. Actually he spent half the day driving and the other half folding the maps. "Why the hell can't they give you a course in college in map-folding? Teach you something useful for a change!" he could be heard yelling at just about every intersection between New York City and Peeksville.

The numbers were getting closer. 651. 655. There! 657. But all joy in finding the place was immediately wiped out by the huge sign that crossed the driveway. Peeksville Home for the Mentally Ill. This was not a good sign. Not a good sign at all. Buddy set his jaw and entered the long driveway.

He stopped in front of what appeared to be the main building. He got out of his car and walked in. The reception desk was not staffed. He rang a little bell that was on the counter. A nurse walked by quickly.

"Excuse me," Buddy called to her. "Do you know where a Lorraine Harden is?"

"Room 106. That way," said the nurse disinterestedly.

Buddy shrugged and headed in the direction she pointed. He had no idea what to expect. How was he going to explain his situation to Maggie's mother? What shape was Maggie's mother in? As he passed by the small private rooms, he realized just how little he really knew about Maggie. Oh, sure, he'd asked her some questions about her family. She'd said her father was dead. She said something about her mother that he couldn't remember, but he was sure she didn't say she was ill. Not like this.

He came to Room 106. The door was slightly ajar. He pushed it open and walked into the room. Standing and looking out the window was an elderly lady with her back to him.

Buddy cleared his throat. "Mrs. Harden?" No response. A little louder perhaps. "Mrs. Harden?"

The woman turned around. She had a face like Ma Barker and a voice that sounded like Burgess Meredith's in *Rocky*. She started to shadow-box.

"It was bee-you-tiful! You shoulda seen it. Da way dey had dat bum pinned to da ropes. I'm telling you. It was bee-you-tiful!"

Buddy stared at her. "Mrs. Harden?"

"Dat's me. What's your business, Buster?"

Oh, God, thought Buddy. This is my son's grand-mother.

"Are you really Mrs. Harden?"

"I yam."

"I, uh, I wanted to talk to you about your daughter Maggie."

"A sweet kid. A hell of a jabber. Good left hook, too. No doubt about it. So," the woman said with a proud smile, "she told you about her old mother?"

"Not quite all, no," said Buddy, wondering if it was too late for prayer.

The old lady stared straight at him. "So?"

"I was hoping you might know her whereabouts."

The woman suddenly became very angry. "What the hell do I care where she is? Huh?"

"Well, I—"

"She's a whore. A slut. A no-good tramp! I don't want to talk about her!"

Buddy stammered. "Well, I see your point, but—"

"Ask her father," snapped the old woman as she started to box against the reflection of the cars in the window.

"I thought he was dead."

"No. He ain't dead. He's in the next room."

Buddy was stunned. "He's here, too?"

"Been here forty years." She yelled into the next room, "Clarence, get your ass out here!"

Buddy stood paralyzed. Her father was an inmate here, too. There was no chance for his son now. And as he thought all this through, the door opened and a small, crumpled black man came through the door. He was stooped and singing "Old Man River" at the top of his voice.

"Old Man River, he just keeps rolling . . ."

Buddy couldn't move. Clarence approached the old woman, and they began to sing together.

". . . he's tired of livin' and 'fraid of dyin' . . ."

Suddenly the door burst open and a middle-aged woman doctor walked quickly up to the two singers.

"Jesse! Clarence! Shut up this moment and go back to your rooms." Silence. The doctor turned to Buddy. "Hello," she said, extending her hand. "I'm Dr. Harden. What can I do for you?"

Buddy said nothing. He just lunged at her and gave her a tight bear hug. Dr. Harden wondered who this madman was and if he was going to let her go.

A half-hour later Buddy sat, having coffee with Dr. Harden in her private office.

"Maggie's a stubborn girl."

"I know," said Buddy. "I know." He quickly surveyed some of the titles of the books on her shelves. He spotted one that he'd read on the subject of child bearing.

"Oh, Peterson's book. I know it well," said Buddy, proud to show some knowledge of psychology.

"Oh, that book. He's a madman. His theories will make children insane."

Buddy's face fell. "Of course. Of course. But I like the, uh, pictures."

"Are you involved with Maggie?"

"In a manner of speaking, yes."

"I seem to have lost touch with her over the past year. Is she all right?"

"She's fine."

This was obviously going to be a standoff of sorts.

Buddy didn't want to say too much, and Dr. Harden didn't want to pry. There was a lot of silent understanding going on and a lot of speaking between the lines.

"I'm afraid I don't know where she is," the doctor said, standing up.

"When I find out, I'll let you know," promised Buddy.

"Please do."

Buddy left the grounds of the "home," feeling much better. Lorraine Harden had a very calming air about her. A reassuring air.

TWENTY-FOUR

Buddy "looked" for Maggie over the next few weeks, but not with the proverbial zeal of a Sherlock Holmes. He wanted to find her. Of that he was sure. He wanted to make sure his son was all right. Of that he was even more sure. But somehow the visit to Dr. Harden's office had given him some perspective. Somehow he knew that he would see Maggie again. In his more pessimistic moments, he hoped that it would be before his son graduated from college.

Maggie, meanwhile, worked at giving music lessons to the millions of untalented New York teenagers. She kept pretty much to herself, occupying the loft in Soho while Smog was playing in Boston. She rested a lot, read a lot, and thought a lot. About Buddy.

One afternoon Kurt's son Tad dropped by the Garden to see his favorite "Uncle" Buddy. Buddy canceled his business meeting and went down to the arena floor to play basketball with the towheaded youngster. Buddy hoped this would get his mind off Maggie and his son, but it didn't. Having Tad around only reminded him of the situation more.

After Buddy missed his tenth shot in a row, Tad spoke up. "Maybe we oughta quit, Uncle Buddy," he suggested, sensing Buddy's mood.

"No way," Buddy replied, doing his best to sound cheery. He dribbled the ball to the foul line. "I'm gonna get one of these suckers in today."

He set himself, shot—and missed by a mile. Neither he nor Tad went after the ball.

"Something wrong?" Tad asked.

"No. Why should something be wrong?"

"Dad says you're upset 'cause Maggie left you."

Buddy regarded the boy's serious face. "Your dad's full of it," he said. "Besides, she didn't leave me. She just left the apartment. She's still in town somewhere."

"Are you gonna marry her?" Tad asked.

"Marry Maggie?" Buddy snorted. "*Me?* Are you kidding or what?"

Tad was still regarding him with the same serious face.

"Why?" Buddy asked him, letting his guard down. "You think I should marry her?"

"I think you *better* marry her."

Buddy was taken aback by Tad's bluntness. "Why should I *better* marry her?"

Tad smiled and pointed to the basketball net. " 'Cause maybe you'd like to sink one of those shots," he replied.

Buddy looked at him for a moment and then broke into a smile. He retrieved the ball and dribbled it back to the free-throw line.

"I'll sink one," Buddy said confidently. "Just watch."

He shot.

He missed.

"Maybe you've got a point there about Maggie," Buddy said to Tad. "I'm getting awfully tired of missing."

TWENTY-FIVE

CELIA HELPED MAGGIE PACK UP THE REST OF HER things. Maggie had called that morning to make sure the coast would be clear—that is, to make sure Buddy wouldn't be around. Celia assured her that there was no chance of his showing up unexpectedly.

"You look like you're gonna deliver any minute, girl," Celia observed. The two of them were in the bedroom, boxing sheet music. "You okay?" Celia could see that Maggie did not look happy.

"I'm fine," Maggie replied. But she looked pale and tired as if she wasn't getting much sleep.

"You been eatin' all right?"

"I've been eating all right."

Celia could take no more. "Now you listen to me," she said, angrily wagging a finger at Maggie. She was determined to speak her mind. "This little game's been goin' on long enough. Why don't you just go up to him and tell him that you love him?"

"Because I *don't* love him," Maggie replied.

"Hey, this is Celia you're talkin' to. I know the score here. A man like Buddy, he needs a shock. Go right up to him and say, 'Buddy, I love you.' "

"But I *don't* love him," Maggie emphasized. She started packing as fast as she could.

Celia approached her and laid a hand on her shoulder. "Maggie," she said softly. "You *do* love him—we both know it."

Maggie's body sagged. She looked at Celia and nodded, "Okay, okay," she admitted. "I *do* love him. Or at least I *did* love him. Somewhere, somewhere way back in my mind, I had this dream that after the baby was born, we'd fall madly in love and I'd be the first person to find out where Buddy's heart is. Now isn't that the dumbest dream you ever heard?"

"Yeah, I think it's dumb," Celia concurred. "But those are the dreams that come true, the dumb ones."

Maggie remained negative. "It's pointless. I'm just going to take me and my baby and go somewhere far away."

"He's gonna find you," Celia warned. "I know that man. That's his baby, and he's got the contract to prove it."

"Screw the damn contract." Maggie started fuming all over again. "You know what I'd like to do, Celia? I'd like to take that damn contract and rip it up into a million tiny pieces." She had a funny look on her face. "As a matter of fact," she exclaimed, "that's exactly what I'm gonna do!"

Maggie strode purposefully out of the room and down the hallway to the closet. She threw it open and began searching through the pockets of one of Buddy's overcoats.

"What're you doin'?" Celia asked, coming upon her.

"He's got a set of keys to his office somewhere in this apartment. He told me once they were here." She turned to Celia with a desperate look. "Where are they, Celia?"

"I can't tell you that," she replied.

"Please, Celia," Maggie asked imploringly.

Celia hesitated. Then she, too, had a funny look on her face. "No way am I tellin' you they're in the writing desk in Buddy's den."

Maggie streaked into the den, followed by Celia.

"It wouldn't be ethical of me to tell you that they were in the drawer," Celia continued. "The top right-hand drawer."

Maggie opened the drawer only to find *several* key rings inside.

"Yes sir," Celia said, "they're gonna stay right on that key ring next to the letter opener."

Maggie picked up the ring. There must have been two dozen keys on it.

"And that gold key next to the little silver one is gonna stay right here in this apartment if *I* have anything to say about it."

"Where's Buddy right now?" Maggie asked.

"He's out of town," Celia replied. "In Los Angeles."

"He is?"

Celia nodded, and Maggie threw her arms around her, giving her a big hug. "I'll come back and get my stuff later," Maggie said. "I think you're wonderful, Celia."

And with that, Maggie rushed out of the room. Celia stood perfectly still in the middle of the den and waited until she heard the front door open and slam shut.

"It's really gonna hit the fan tonight," she said with a wicked smile.

In his office, Buddy was commiserating with Larry over a bottle of Scotch. They'd been at it for nearly an hour, and neither was feeling any pain.

"A private detective?" Larry chortled and poured himself another shot. "Are you kidding?"

"I've got to find her," Buddy said flatly. He meant it, too. "She's got my damned baby."

"The girl's in love, you numbskull," Larry pointed out. "Haven't you ever been in love before?"

"No," Buddy replied emphatically. "But then again, you're talking to a man who's never had the mumps . . . can't blow a bubble . . . hates the Beatles . . . and has never seen *Fantasia* stoned. And what the hell do you mean by 'before' anyway? You said haven't I ever been in love *before!*"

"For God's sake, Buddy, just come out and say it."

"Say what?"

"Say you love her."

Buddy put his glass down. "I *love* her?"

"It's not so hard," Larry informed him. "Try it one word at a time. I—love—"

They were both startled from their slouching positions as the door suddenly swung open and Maggie came into the room. As soon as she saw Buddy behind the desk, she froze.

"Maggie!" Buddy cried, his face lighting up with delight. He stood and knocked over the Scotch bottle, but didn't even notice it.

"Celia said you were in Los Angeles," Maggie sputtered in surprise.

"Where'd she get an idea like that?" Buddy wondered. "She knew I'd be *here* all day."

They both realized in the same instant that Celia had set them up. Maggie heard the door shut behind her. Turning, she saw Larry throwing the lock.

"The two of you are going to stay right here until you work this out," he stated and leaned his back against the door.

"He's right, Maggie," said Buddy, starting around the desk toward her. "We have to talk."

"Don't come any closer," she warned.

"Did you miss me?"

"That's not the point."

"What is?"

"I'm keeping this baby," Maggie announced. "I'm keeping it, and that's all there is to it."

"It's my baby, too," Buddy argued.

"I realize that," Maggie nodded. "I'm willing to make you an offer."

"What kind of offer?"

"A compromise."

"What kind of compromise?"

Maggie reached into her overcoat pocket and pulled out a pocket calendar. "You can have visiting rights."

"Visiting rights?"

"Once a month, New Year's Day, better take Memorial Day, too—"

"Hey," Larry interrupted. "Why don't you two knock off the bullshit? Buddy, you start."

"Start what?" he asked innocently.

"Just one word at a time," Larry instructed. "Repeat after me. 'I . . . love . . . you . . . Maggie.' Go on."

"What's he talking about?" Maggie asked Buddy.

"Say it," Larry urged.

Buddy took a deep breath. He stepped forward and gripped Maggie by the shoulders. "Maggie," he began, his voice beginning to falter. "Maggie . . ."

"What?"

"Maggie, I love you!" he shouted and turned away, too embarrassed to face her.

"Do you really?" Maggie asked in a small voice.

Buddy nodded. "I have for a long time," he confessed. "And not just because of the baby. I really do love you, Maggie."

Maggie took a couple of uneasy steps backwards and touched a hand to her forehead. Her eyelids suddenly fluttered, and her knees buckled. Luckily, Larry was close enough to catch her and help her down into a chair.

"I guess I really took her breath away," Buddy observed.

"The *baby* took her breath away," Larry said. "Maggie . . . how do you feel, honey?"

Maggie regained her composure, but her face was flushed. "I think it's time," she said with a weak smile.

"*Time?*" Buddy echoed, suddenly nervous. He looked at his watch. "Time for what?"

"Time to get this young lady to the hospital," Larry answered.

"You mean she's going to have the baby?" Buddy gulped. He felt his own knees growing weak.

"She's going to have it right here if we don't get moving." Larry helped Maggie up and steered her toward the door. "You call ahead and we'll meet you there," he shouted over his shoulder as they went out.

Buddy nodded and fumbled for the phone. It fell to the floor, and he had to get down on all fours to retrieve it from under the desk. Just as he stood up and started to dial, Kurt rushed into the room.

"Is she gonna have the baby?" he asked rhetorically.

Buddy thrust the phone at him. "Here, you call." He grabbed his overcoat and started to put it on—backwards. "And after you do that, I want you to call Celia."

"What for?"

"To make arrangements," Buddy replied, trying to get his arms out of the wrong sleeves. "There's something we have to do before the baby arrives."

The maternity wing was congested to begin with, so when Buddy stepped off the elevator with *his* party in tow, it only added to the general confusion. Aside from Kurt and Larry, he was accompanied by Celia and a tall, dignified black gentleman.

"Follow me," Buddy ordered like a squad captain and lead them down a corridor that was already bustling with patients, visitors, and staff. "Her room's right down here."

"Hey, Buddy, keep it down," said Larry, noticing that they were attracting attention. "This is a hospital."

Celia quickened her stride and gravitated alongside Buddy. "I guess I gotta hand it to ya," she said begrudgingly. "For the first time in your life, you're doin' the right thing—crazy but right."

Buddy looked like John Wayne heading down Main Street on his way to a showdown. Because of the purposeful nature of his stride and the intense look on his face, a number of the patients and visitors who were lingering in the hall began to follow behind out of curiosity. This caught the attention of the nursing staff who then fell in behind in order to investigate. By the time Buddy reached Maggie's room, he had assembled quite a crowd.

He was about to enter when Maggie was suddenly thrust through the door and into the hall on a gurney. She had begun labor.

"Maggie!" Buddy cried out in concern.

"What's going on here?" the attending doctor demanded. He was less than delighted with the crowd that was now clogging the corridor.

"We're getting married," Buddy replied.

"*Now?*" the doctor looked at him as if he were a madman. "She's going to have a *baby!*"

"It's okay, Bill," Larry assured the doctor. "It'll only take a second."

Buddy bent down and spoke softly but urgently into Maggie's ear. "Maggie? It's me—Buddy."

"Buddy?" There was a faraway quality to her voice.

"I have something to ask you."

"Ask me what?" she managed, trying to focus her eyes on him.

"Maggie," Buddy swallowed hard. He reached over and took her hand in his. "Will you . . . *marry* me?"

Her eyes opened wide with surprise, and suddenly she had no trouble focusing. She turned her head to look at him. "Do you mean that?" she demanded.

"Yeah," Buddy smiled. "Of course I mean it."

Maggie grinned back. "You'd be breaking the contract . . ."

"Screw the contract!" he replied. "What do you say? Will you marry me?"

Maggie let out a sudden scream of pain.

"Is that a yes or a no?" Buddy asked desperately.

"It's a yes," Maggie answered once the pain had passed.

Buddy turned excitedly to the surrounding throng. "She said yes," he announced. "She's gonna marry me!"

The crowd cheered its approval.

"Okay, Reverend," Buddy said to the dignified gentleman beside Celia.

"Mr. Evans, we can't wait much longer," the doctor said.

A look of terror suddenly crossed Buddy's face. "Rings," he cried. "We don't have any rings!"

"I've got one," Kurt said, yanking one off his finger.

"Here's another," added Larry, taking off his.

"Terrific," Buddy said and pulled Celia over. "You be maid of honor."

"What about music?" asked a woman in the crowd. "What's a wedding without music?"

"She's right," Buddy said, then got a flash of an idea. He addressed the crowd. "Everybody hum! Hum 'The Wedding March.' "

Cooperatively, the crowd began to do just that. Buddy stood beside Maggie lying on the gurney. "Okay," he said to the reverend. "Shoot."

The reverend stepped up and opened his Bible. "Guess I better do the *Reader's Digest* version," he suggested, looking at Maggie. "Do you, Maggie, take this man to be—"

"I do!"

"And do you, Buddy, take this—"

"I do!"

"Then by the power vested in me, I now pronounce you man and wife."

The crowd broke into cheers and applause. Buddy moved his mouth to Maggie's and kissed her. They held the kiss until the doctor broke them up. "Sorry, you two," the doctor said, brushing a tear from his eye, "but we've got a baby to deliver."

"I love you," Buddy said, squeezing her hand.

"I love *you*," Maggie replied, then suddenly let out another scream.

The doctor moved Buddy aside as the attendants wheeled Maggie down the hall and through the doors of the delivery room. Buddy made his way through the throng of happy strangers over to Kurt and Larry. They both had broad grins on their faces. Buddy had one of his own.

"I'm married," he exclaimed, and unable to contain his joy, he threw his arms around them both.

"Well," Kurt mused, "I for one never thought I'd see the day."

"Buddy Evans—an old married man," Larry chuckled. "And unless I miss my guess, you're also going to be a father any minute now."

Buddy nodded. "I've got everything I ever wanted," he said, unaware of the tears that were forming in his eyes. "A woman I love—and a *son*."

TWENTY-SIX

IN HER ROOM MAGGIE LAY IN BED, SMILING UP AT THE beaming father.

Buddy kept shaking his head. "She's the most beautiful little girl I ever saw."

Maggie agreed. "She is."

Buddy took his wife's hand. "I love you both."

"I love you both, too."

"And this is just the start. God, we have so much ahead of us." Buddy walked around in a little circle, not sure what to do with all the happiness he was experiencing. Suddenly he stopped. He turned, snapping his fingers as if getting a wonderful idea.

"You know what would be terrific?"

Maggie imagined great places for the honeymoon.

But Buddy just nodded. "Grandchildren!" His smile grew huge as Maggie looked at him in disbelief and held the baby girl next to her a little tighter.

CONGO

The National Bestseller by

MICHAEL CRICHTON

Author of THE ANDROMEDA STRAIN

"Darkest Africa. Strangling vines. Rain forest. Pygmies. Clouds of mosquitoes. Rampaging hippos. Roaring gorillas. Killer natives. Gorges. Rapids. Erupting volcanoes. An abandoned city full of diamonds, lost in the jungle. Maybe a new animal species, a weird cross between man and ape, but unheard of in 20th-century anthropology. Zaire. Congo. Michael Crichton's newest thriller. And of course: technology, which is what it's all about today, isn't it? Zoom!"

The Boston Globe

"A gem of a thriller!"

Playboy

"Oh, is this ever a good one!"

Detroit News

"The master of very tall tales plunges into the heart of darkness. . . . A dazzling example of how to combine science and adventure writing."

People

"What entertainment! . . . Crichton has created in Amy a 'talking gorilla' of enough charm to enshrine her in pop culture as firmly as R2D2."

Saturday Review

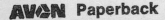 **Paperback**   56176 • $2.95

Congo 10-81